To my dearest readers:

Triple Crown Publications provides you with the best reads in hip-hop fiction. Each novel is hand-selected in its purest form with you, the reader, in mind. *Let That Be the Reason*, an insta-classic, pioneered the hip-hop genre. Always innovative, you can count on Triple Crown's growth: manuscript notes — published books — audio — film.

Triple Crown has also gone international, with novels distributed around the globe. In Tokyo, the books have been translated into Japanese. Triple Crown's revolutionary brand has garnered attention from prominent news media, with features in ABC News, The New York Times, Newsweek, MTV, Publisher's Weekly, The Boston Globe, Vibe, Essence, Entrepreneur Magazine, Inc Magazine, Black Enterprise Magazine, The Washington Post, Millionaire Blueprints Magazine and Writer's Digest, just to name a few. I recently earned Ball State University's Ascent Award for Entrepreneurial Business Excellence and was named by Book Magazine as one of publishing's 50 most influential women. Those prestigious honors have taken me from street corner to boardroom accreditation.

Undisputedly, Triple Crown is the leader of the urban fiction renaissance, boasting more than one million sizzling books sold and counting...

Without you, our readers, there is no us,

Vickie Stringer
Publisher

Betrayed

by David Givens

Compilation and Introduction copyright © 2008 by
Triple Crown Publications
PO Box 6888
Columbus, Ohio 43205
www.TripleCrownPublications.com

Library of Congress Control Number: 2008928912
ISBN 13: 978-0-9799517-7-0
Author: David Givens
Cover Design/Graphics: www.MarionDesigns.com
Typesetting: Holscher Type and Design
Editorial Assistant: Dany Ferneau
Editor-in-Chief: Mia McPherson
Consulting: Vickie M. Stringer

First Trade Paperback Edition Printing May 2008

10 9 8 7 6 5 4 3 2 1

Printed in the United States of America

acknowledgements

First, I would like to thank Allah for blessing a simple guy like me with the opportunity to write a book. It wasn't easy, and at times I wondered what I was doing. Thanks for letting my jumbled thoughts come out into a somewhat understandable manuscript.

I'd like to thank my mother, Denise, for being my friend as well as my mother. We haven't always had the relationship I wanted, but time heals all wounds. To my father, David, I say hopefully we can spend more time together in the future. Thanks to my brothers and sisters, Darius, Sharee, Darvel and Tedniesha. I love you knuckleheads!

Of course I have to thank my children, Davion, Yasmeen, Nasir, Kalilia and Samadiah. You are the lights of my world and the reasons why I write.

And to Sharon, my Queen and the love of my life, I'd like to say thank you for putting up with a crazy guy like me. You are my better half in so many ways.

I would also like to thank my ex-wife and babymomma, Tanzania and Rebecca for giving me such wonderful children.

Special thanks to the Givens, Sisk and Robinson family. That's my peoples. I especially want to thank Rachael Patterson, Naomi Sisk, Chet Sisk, and his family, Wade Sisk and his family, Rodney Sisk, Vania Sisk, Katie Sisk, Ruby Sisk, Marvin Sisk, Willie Sisk, Jermaine Sisk, Danny Muhammad, Shatesia Bruce, David Givens Sr. and Jr., Barbara Givens, Mike Givens, and Rhondalynn Givens. Anyone that I forgot hit me up with a note and I'll get you next time.

I also want to thank my closest friends: Jamieson Harris, Carla Harris, Carolynn Harris, Leverene and Linda Harris, Vincent Harris, Anthony Harris, Tre Williams, Destiny Gardner, Recole Cook, Nakia VanArsdale, Nakeisha Davis, Jackie Carislie, Jennifer Johnson, Brian Lipsey, Marcus Kilgore, Tresha Levell, Valerie Nyberg and Tim Carr. If I forgot you, I'll get you next time.

A special thanks to Shawn Hook and Tyson Fresh Meats. Thanks for the time off to write and for being so understanding.

I would also like to thank all the staff at Triple Crown Publications. I'm glad you took a chance on a nobody like me. I hope I can do you proud.

Thank you to Ms. Vickie Stringer for giving people like me an opportunity to express ourselves. You are truly one in a million. And a special thank you to Mia McPherson and Danielle Ferneau for the editing help.

And last, but not least, the fans!!! Thank you for reading my work. It may be a little rough, but bear with me. It's my first book. I'm bound to get better with time.

Until next time,
D.A. Givens

1

Monday started off on the wrong foot for Darrell "The Sandman" Jenkins. He was awakened by his ringing cell phone at 5 a.m. Normally he wouldn't have answered it, but some fool kept calling him back to back. It turned out that the fool in question was his insane baby momma, Keke. She told him it was an emergency and that he needed to get over to her place right away.

Of course Darrell assumed the emergency involved his three-year-old son, Darrell Jr. He quickly threw on some sweats and hopped into his SUV. The normal 20 minute drive across town took him seven minutes flat. He screeched to a halt in the driveway of Keke's rundown duplex on the lower east side of Waterloo. His long stride had him at the front door in a flash.

David Givens

The door was open and the lights appeared to be off. Darrell pulled out the chrome 9mm handgun he usually kept in his waistband and proceeded inside with caution. The living room was dark and quiet. Everything appeared to be in its place. He called Keke's name, but received no answer. The kitchen and lower bathroom were dark and empty also. Sweat started to bead up on Darrell's forehead. He wiped it away as he headed up the stairs to the bedrooms.

He checked his son's room first and was relieved not to find him dead or injured. However, where was he? No one would be stupid enough to kidnap his son. That would be suicide. He proceeded to check the spare bedroom and the hallway closets next. Everything seemed normal. When he got to the upstairs bathroom he noticed the mirror was still fogged over from someone's recent shower. That someone only had one other place to hide in the house.

The last room down the hallway was Keke's. He approached it with trepidation. There was no telling what horror lay hidden behind the door. Darrell braced himself as he kicked the door open and charged in with his gun leading the way.

The sight before him was so absurd that he almost busted off a few shots accidentally. The room was bathed in candlelight and smelled of jasmine. Keke lay

David Givens

in the middle of her queen sized bed butt-ass naked, surrounded by rose petals. Her milk chocolate skin was flawless. She smiled a wicked smile at him and opened her legs.

Her pussy was shaved and wet. She opened the pink lips so he could get a better view. Then she inserted a finger in ever so slowly. "Take me, big daddy," she moaned as she massaged her clit. She opened her eyes only to see that Darrell was nowhere to be found.

Darrell stormed out of the room in a rage. The nerve of that bitch, getting him all riled up early in the morning just because she wanted a booty call. He wasn't some pussy whipped motherfucker ready to fuck at her beck and call. Sometimes he wished he never fucked with her in the first place.

"Darrell, I know you aren't about to just leave me here like this. You know you want it just as bad as I do."

He turned and saw her naked silhouette framed in the doorway. They locked eyes for what seemed like an eternity. Finally, Darrell stalked toward her like an enraged lion. He kissed her roughly at the door and pushed her back into the hallway. His heavily muscled six foot three frame towered over her. He grabbed her by the throat and pinned her up against the wall. He shoved his 9mm in her face.

Keke's hot pink tongue flicked out and licked the

David Givens

barrel seductively. Darrell let her go and threw his gun on the couch. Keke was on her knees in a flash tugging at his sweatpants. She pulled them and his silk boxers down to his ankles. His huge dick stood at attention like a good soldier. She hungrily took it into her warm mouth. Darrell's eyes rolled back into his head as he let her do her thing.

Her head game was vicious and on point. She swirled her tongue around the tip of his swollen member a few times before licking up and down all nine inches of his shaft. Then she took as much of him into her mouth as she could. Her free hand caressed his balls as she sucked and licked him into ecstasy.

When he was ready he pulled her to her feet and turned her around to face the wall. He entered her savagely from behind. His dick pounded her pussy like Barry Bonds connecting on a fast ball. Keke skillfully grinded back into him hard, as if she was trying to become one with him. He alternated between pulling her expensive weave and slapping her round ghetto ass.

Then he pulled her to the floor and flipped her over. He placed her legs on his broad shoulders and rammed into her deep and slow. She scratched at his back and thrashed her head back and forth wildly. Tears streamed from her eyes like water from a leaky faucet.

David Givens

This was thug passion at its best. Hot, dirty and rough.

"Oh God I'm coming," said Keke as she tensed up.

Darrell started grinding his dick into her harder and faster. They came together in one explosive orgasm and collapsed into a heap on the floor. Darrell rolled off her and pulled his sweatpants back up. She lay on the floor breathing heavily with a satisfied smile on her face. He loved her and hated her all at the same time.

"So where is my son?" Darrell asked when he caught his breath.

"He's away at his grandparents'. I thought we could use some time alone together," Keke said as she traced the wave patterns in his perfectly trimmed fade.

"Keke, you know what we had is long over. I never move backwards. You fucked up so now deal with it."

"What was this then? You know you can't get enough of me. No one can put it on you like me, nigga."

Darrell shook his head and got to his feet. Keke always thought sex could solve everything. Nothing could change the fact that she was a ghetto nympho that cheated on him when they were together. Back then he was just a small time hustler that didn't make enough money to keep her satisfied. Now that he was running things she thought she could slip back into the picture. If she wasn't the mother of his son he wouldn't even be bothered with her. He grabbed his gun off the couch and headed for the door.

"Where the fuck are you going? You just gonna leave me like that? I'm talking to you, motherfucker."

Darrell didn't answer her. The fucking he gave her was all the goodbye she would receive. Keke got off the floor and rushed at him screaming every curse word she could think of. She grabbed his arm as he reached the doorway. He whirled on her quickly and she could see the fire burning in his intense brown eyes. She backed away quietly with fear written all over her face.

Darrell wasn't called the Sandman for nothing. Niggas who fucked with him usually ended up being put to sleep permanently. His rep was well known in the streets. Even a foul-mouthed ghetto girl like Keke had to respect his gangster. She knew she could only push him so far. Maybe it was time to cut her losses and give up. At least she would still be tied to him by their son.

Darrell walked out to his brand new black Lexus truck and opened the door. He saw Keke admiring the huge 26 inch chromed out wheels his vehicle sat on. If she would have played her part right then she would be in the passenger seat. Instead she was on the outside looking in. It served her gold digging ass right. Maybe she would treat the next man better. Somehow he doubted that. For now she would just have to deal with

David Givens

the thousand dollars he was giving her every month for their son.

He started his engine up and pulled off. It was still early, but the grind waited for no man. Making money would get his mind off Keke's trifling ass. He lit up an Optimo blunt, filled with the finest ganja from Cali, and took a long drag. The latest album by Nas pumped through his speakers at full blast. He lost himself in the music as he drove down the block. Just another crazy morning in the life of a hustler.

2

Two hours later, Darrell had showered, shaved and changed into a chocolate short-sleeved linen outfit. He was back out cruising in his Lexus with a freshly lit blunt clutched between his teeth. Its smoke swirled around him like his thoughts were swirling around in his head at the moment. The episode with Keke earlier had messed with him far more than he wanted to let on.

For almost two years they were the perfect couple. They met his senior year in high school. At the time he was a high school football standout. No one could tackle harder than the Sandman. That is until one day he blew his knee out. The scouts disappeared on him like Houdini; on to the next black boy with talent.

Keke had stayed with him regardless. He started

hustling soon after he graduated. Everyone told him that Keke was no good, but all he could see was the way her eyes lit up when he came in from the block with pockets full of money. She kept him fed and supplied him with mind blowing sex on the regular. So what if she spent up money like water?

After their son was born she started going out more and more. He would come home to an empty house with no food on the stove. Their son would always be with relatives. Her spending habits had gotten out of control. Money started coming up missing. Darrell let it slide for a while because he loved her.

Then rumors of her cheating on him began to circulate. He didn't want to believe them at first. However, she was staying out later and later. One day he came home early to grab his basketball sneakers for a pick up game and got the shock of his life. He saw a brand new Benz sitting in their driveway. It made his three-year-old Toyota Camry sitting on 20s look ordinary.

He came in the duplex and walked up to the main bedroom just like he did a few hours ago. The door was closed then, too. Sounds were coming from the other side of the door that would make a prostitute blush. He had opened the door to find Keke on her back moaning with his boss, Big Rome's face buried between her legs.

Big Rome was Darrell's mentor and the man that

put him on in the game. He was the top dope man in the city at the time. A man you didn't mess with. So what if he was giving it to Darrell's girl? The best thing to do would have been to quietly exit the room and pretend that he hadn't seen it; however Darrell wasn't a man to be messed with either.

He stormed the room and proceeded to bounce Big Rome off the walls like a ping-pong ball. Big Rome was bigger than Darrell, but he was out of shape and exhausted from sexing all afternoon. He ended up with a broken arm, broken jaw, two black eyes and three cracked ribs. Darrell packed his shit and got out while Rome lay on the floor gasping for air like a fish out of water. Keke just sat in the bed looking like a deer caught in the headlights.

Big Rome put a hit out on him after he got out of surgery, but Darrell didn't have any intentions of running. Four of Big Rome's boys caught up to him in a bar later on that night. After the smoke cleared, Darrell was the only one left standing. Soon afterwards Big Rome was found suffocated in his hospital bed.

Darrell started the Get Money Crew, or GMC, soon after that. He took over Big Rome's top spot in the city after three months of violence and bloodshed. Now his legend was cemented in the hood. No cocaine moved in the city without him knowing about it. He was a

David Givens

baller now who played hoes like dominoes. He had Keke to thank for that. In her own misguided way she had put him on top. However, she also planted the seeds of mistrust toward females in him. He vowed to never let a woman get too close to him ever again.

His vibrating cell phone brought his attention back to the present. His boy, Terry, was hitting him up. Terry Law was Darrell's best friend. They went back like Lemonheads and Chick-O-Sticks. Terry was his right hand man in the GMC and had his back all the way.

"What's good Sandman, where you at?"

"I'm on Ankeny close to Sullivan Park."

"Alright, I'm a few blocks away. I'll meet you at the park, one."

Darrell pulled over to the curb at Sullivan Park. He got out of his vehicle and wiped a smudge off his chocolate crocodile Stacy Adams before walking over to a park bench to sit down. A few sistas sitting at a picnic table nearby stopped their conversation to stare at him. Darrell was two hundred and forty pounds of rippling muscles and tattoos. His skin was the color of polished ebony and his teeth sparkled Colgate white. Women loved him and men respected him.

He smiled at the sistas and let them see his dimples. They giggled and looked away. If he didn't have business to tend to at the moment he would have been over at their table putting his mack down. Instead he nodded at them and proceeded to check the organizer on his cell phone.

A few minutes later he heard the sound of a loud car stereo system throbbing heavy with bass. The bass was so heavy that everyone within a three block radius stopped what they were doing and car alarms started going off. A large candy apple red H2 Hummer turned the corner at a high rate of speed. The earthquake-inducing bass was coming from it. It slowed down as it approached the park, but it didn't stop. Instead it jumped the curb and drove through the grass toward Darrell.

The sistas who were nearby got up and moved away quickly like they thought a drive by was about to go down. Darrell just folded his arms and smirked. The H2 stopped about two feet in front of him and the music cut off. The engine revved a few times then the driver's door opened. His boy Terry jumped out with a grin on his face.

Terry was a small light-skinned brother around five-foot-nine. He had a lean build and a flashy demeanor. Most women thought he resembled T.I. He was dressed in a white beater, blue Sean John jeans and some vintage white and red Jordans. His watch, rings and the many chains that hung around his neck were made of

David Givens

platinum and encrusted with hundreds of colorful diamonds. He was a baller in every sense of the word.

"Yo, you like my new toy? I got like six televisions
in that bitch and I know you heard that system," Terry
said as he gave Darrell some dap.

"Are those thirty inch wheels you sitting on?"
Darrell asked as he checked out the giant rims gleam-
ing in the sunlight.

"Bigger is better homie, bigger is better."

Darrell could only shake his head and laugh. He and
Terry were as different as night and day. Terry was over
the top and grimey as fuck. He was loud, arrogant and
dangerous. The kind of brother who let his guns do the
talking. Darrell was more reserved and low-key. He
didn't show his power unless he had to. That's why he
was respected by both enemies and friends while Terry
was feared by all.

Both friends sat down on the bench and got down
to business. Terry filled Darrell in on how everything
was running. He told him of the money he had already
collected that morning and of the money he projected
they would make this coming week. Darrell always let
Terry handle their dealers and the collection of money
owed to them. He was more focused on dealing with
their contacts and making their illegal money into legit
money.

David Givens

"There is something I did want to talk to you about, homie." Terry's face got serious for a moment. "Ray Ray came up short again."

Ray Ray was Terry's first cousin. He had only been in the GMC for two months, but he was already costing them more money than he was worth. He was always coming up short and thinking he would get a pass because Terry was his cousin. Darrell was going to address the matter, but he was glad Terry beat him to the punch. Especially since he was the one that was going to have to deal with him.

"How much this time?" Darrell asked.

"Two grand."

Darrell's right eyebrow shot up almost a full inch. That motherfucker was either stealing from them or getting high off the stuff he was supposed to be selling. Either way he was going to be dealt with severely. Messing with his money was like slapping him in the face. He turned his blazing eyes toward Terry.

"Deal with it. Do you have a problem with that?"

"Naw man, I'm on it," said Terry, returning Darrell's stare. He hated when anyone barked orders at him, but he wasn't about to argue. Besides he knew he was going to have to deal with his cousin one day. It was a mistake putting him on in the first place. Business and family didn't always mix.

David Givens

"So what about those L-Block Boys?" Terry asked, changing the subject.

The L-Block Boys were a new gang in town that had sprung up within the last year. They usually operated on the upper east side, around Logan Avenue. At first they only slang a little weed and X here and there, but now they were trying to break into the dope game. Unlike the other small gangs in the city, they weren't trying to cut the GMC in on their share. There had been a few run-ins between the crews at local bars, but nothing major had popped off.

"They are nothing but a bunch of coked up young fools with itchy trigger fingers. We'll have to shut them down soon. However, I'm more concerned with who is behind them. They are too stupid to get into the dope game without some help. Have some of the boys hit the streets and find out who they're connected to."

"I'll get Loco and Jay on that right away. Let me hit you off with this package before I go," said Terry as he got up and headed back to his H2.

He opened the back door on the driver's side and grabbed a black duffle bag which he tossed to Darrell. They gave each other dap again and Darrell walked off toward his Lexus. He opened his door and threw the bag into the passenger seat. Then he got in and unzipped the bag. There was around thirty thousand dollars in stacks of one hundred dollar bills. Not bad for a Monday morning. They would make twice that amount by nightfall. Darrell smiled and zipped the bag back up. Today was shaping up to be a good day after all.

Terry sat in his H2 and watched Darrell pull off. He reached under his seat and grabbed his .45 handgun. It was loaded and ready for action. The cold steel felt great in his palm. He placed it in his waistband and reached into his hidden stash box under his dashboard and pulled out a small vial of coke. One snort up each nostril and he was on cloud nine. He sped out of the park on his way to see Ray Ray. He left a trail of ripped up grass and dirt in his wake.

David Givens

3

Sherrice Valdez was officially sick of her life. Nothing seemed to be going right for her as of late. She had slept through her alarm that morning and had needed a fifteen full minutes to start up her rusty old hoopty. Now she was standing in front of her manager who was yelling at her for being late once again. She didn't need this drama.

"Look at me when I'm talking to you, Sherrice. Do you know the value of being on time?" asked her pimple-faced manager. He wore a too tight white short sleeved shirt with a small neck tie that looked like it was choking him. His face was beet red and just plain ugly.

"What you need to do is get out my face. I said I was sorry," said Sherrice as she rolled her green eyes and sucked her teeth.

"No, what you need to do is get out of my restaurant. I'm tired of your attitude. You're fired. Turn your apron in on your way out."

"Fuck you and this lame-ass job. I don't need this shit." She took off her apron and threw it in the manager's face. She brushed past him hurriedly almost knocking him to the ground.

When she got outside, she stopped in front of her car and kicked the front tire until she couldn't lift her leg anymore. Then she got behind the wheel and started to cry.

Life wasn't supposed to be this hard. If only she wouldn't have dropped out of high school. Back then she didn't have a care in the world. She was too fly for that education shit. Her foster mother had tried to warn her, but she had laughed in the old woman's face. Now she was a nineteen-year-old recently unemployed sista struggling to survive.

Sherrice wiped her eyes and fought to regain control of herself. She wasn't a quitter. Maybe it was time to use the beauty that God gave her to get what she wanted. All of her girlfriends were using sex to get money out of the many ballers in the city. Maybe it was time for her to start doing the same. It was either do that or become a stripper. Neither option appealed that

David Givens

much to her, but she needed to do something fast.

She tried a couple times to start her car, but it just wasn't moving. The engine was finally shot. Nothing was going her way today. She took a deep breath and got out of the car. A nice walk would do her some good anyway.

Even dressed down for work, Sherrice was beautiful. Her skin was blemish free and a smooth caramel color. Her nice cantaloupe-sized breasts defied gravity without needing a bra. The low cut jeans she wore hugged her nice shapely hips and showed off her perfectly round ass. Years of running track, before she quit school, had given her a nice lean build with a pair of sculpted abs and stunning legs. She also had long silky auburn hair that hung down to the middle of her back.

What really drove the guys crazy however, were her nice full lips and her mysterious green eyes. Her looks were a product of a Brazilian father she never knew and an African-American mother who died of a heroin overdose when she was four. Sherrice always knew she looked exotic, but she never dated that many guys. In fact, she had only had two boyfriends in her entire life. This made cats in the streets want to get at her even more.

She started walking down the street clutching her imitation Louis Vuitton purse. Her apartment was two miles away, over in the ghetto. It was the morning time so she didn't have to worry too much about being hassled. Most thugs were still sleeping off the booze they drank the night before. At least she had her comfortable sneakers on.

Sherrice admired the scenery around her as she walked home. Her job was located in a nice middle class neighborhood. The lawns were taken care of and the houses were decent looking. She wished she had grown up in one of those houses. Instead she had to grow up with a foster mother who was jealous of her looks and an older foster brother who liked to try and play grab ass with her in the middle of the night. He learned his lesson when she kicked him in the nuts and clawed his face up.

Sherrice looked up and realized she was almost home. The buildings around her started to get more rundown and the lawns were either overgrown with weeds or littered with patches of dirt and garbage. Broken glass crunched under her feet. The ghettos were the same everywhere you went—nothing but decay and struggle.

The sound of a car pulling up to the curb made her turn her head. She noticed a hunter green Chevy Tahoe with heavily tinted windows. The passenger window rolled down and she found herself staring right into the

David Givens

face of J-Ice and a few of his homies. He smiled at her showing off his gold and diamond grill.

"What's up, shortie. You need a ride?" asked the leader of the L-Block Boys.

"Naw, I'm cool. I only live a block away," said Sherrice walking a little faster.

"Well can I give you a ride somewhere else then?"

"I don't think so. You have a good day." Sherrice dismissed him with a wave of her hand. She knew she shouldn't have done it, but she was still feeling pissed off about losing her job. Besides she wasn't about to go anywhere with J-Ice's fat, short ass.

The brother in the passenger seat let out a small laugh and J-Ice popped him in the mouth. He drove his Tahoe up on the sidewalk in front of Sherrice blocking her path. Then he jumped out with a black 9mm in his hand. He walked up on her fast and grabbed her arm. The gun was pointed at her head.

"You think you too good for me, bitch?" His breath smelled of Olde English malt liquor and weed.

"So you just gonna shoot me for not giving you no play? The mighty J-Ice got to shoot bitches for dates now?" asked Sherrice. She was scared out of her mind, but that didn't stop her from popping off at the mouth. Her mouth always had a mind of its own and today was no different.

David Givens

J-Ice stared at her for a minute and then stared back at his boys in the truck. Everything had gone silent. Then he looked back at her again and smiled. He released her arm and started to laugh.

"This bitch is crazy," said J-Ice as he stuffed his gun in the front of his jeans. Then he grabbed her again and whispered in her ear. "I like your style, shortie, but you ain't too cute to get shot. I'll be seeing you around."

Sherrice breathed a sigh a relief as she watched J-Ice and his boys pull off. Her heart was throbbing loud in her ears. Just turning niggas down for dates was getting dangerous now. God, she wished she could get out of the hood.

She approached her apartment building longing to lay down and take a nap. The morning had already taken a lot out of her. She opened the front door to the building and was immediately overwhelmed with the smell of piss, vomit and weed in the hallway. Broken toys, smashed beer cans and condoms were strewn about the floor. The white landlord rarely came out unless someone was behind on rent. Even then, he wouldn't clean the place.

Sherrice entered her second story apartment and placed her purse on the kitchen counter. The place smelled of weed and sex. The sound of moaning and squeaky bedsprings floated to her from the back of the

David Givens

apartment. That meant her roommate, Lashay, was home and she definitely had company.

Lashay and Sherrice had met in high school on the track team. They both had dropped out around the same time and decided to live together so they could keep costs down. Sherrice chose the nine to five route while Lashay was a straight up golddigger. When Lashay wasn't stripping she was usually fucking some baller intent on him tricking his dough off on her. Apparently, she had another victim in her bed.

Sherrice went to the fridge and got out a beer. She twisted the cap off the bottle and started sipping. It was early, but she needed it. Her feet hurt so she took her sneakers off. She made her way down the hallway toward her room hoping Lashay's door wasn't open when she passed. Of course it happened to be open when she came upon it. That's just what type of day it was.

She tried to sneak by without looking, but she found her head turning anyway. Lashay was naked, covered with sweat, riding on top of some grimey cat who hadn't even bothered to take his Timberlands off in the bed. Her 34DD breasts bounced up and down like two chocolate covered basketballs. The guy's hands gripped her huge heart shaped ass helping to guide it up and down. Their pace was fast and furious.

David Givens

Sherrice froze in her tracks and couldn't help but to watch. The sweat on Lashay's dark chocolate skin made it glisten in the sunlight coming through the half-closed blinds. The moaning and the sound of flesh on flesh contact turned her on slightly. She bit her lip and her free hand caressed one of her erect nipples through the thin material of her shirt. It had been so long since she had any dick.

Her left hand traveled down her body to the crotch area of her jeans. Her wet pussy throbbed beneath her clothing. She suddenly felt very warm and lightheaded. The beer bottle in her right hand suddenly slipped out of her grasp. It hit the carpet with at small thud and ruined the fantasy.

It also caught the attention of her roommate and the thug she was screwing. They all looked at each other in silence. Sherrice could feel her face getting hot and turning red. She took her hand off her crotch and placed it behind her back. Lashay smiled at her.

"What's up girl, I thought you were at work?" asked Lashay as she still slowly grinded on top of her friend.

"Naw, I quit that slavery-ass shit. I'm thinking about coming down to the club where you at," Sherrice said, slowly inching away.

"That's cool, girl. It's about time you came to get some real money anyway." Lashay started getting back

David Givens

into her grove for a minute then she turned back to Sherrice. "Hey, you want to join us?"

Sherrice was too shocked to say anything for a moment. She stared back at Lashay and then at the guy she was fucking. His lean body was riddled with scars and old bullet wounds—a true street soldier. She had never been in a threesome before and she wasn't about to get into one with Lashay. They were cool, but not that cool.

"Naw, I'm good. Y'all knock yourselves' out," Sherrice said as she hurriedly picked up her half-spilt beer and beat a hasty retreat to her room. She saw the look of disappointment on the thug's face as she left. He probably thought it was his lucky day. He was just going to have to settle for one girl.

Sherrice closed her bedroom door and sat down on her bed. She was tripping so bad. For a moment she had actually considered joining Lashay and her friend. Now she really knew she needed some dick in her life. It had been at least six months since she had been with a man.

It wasn't that she couldn't get any. Men were spitting game at her all the time. She just wasn't trying to have her name out there in the streets. Once brothers labeled you a ho or golddigger it was over. No decent brother was trying to wife someone like that. You would always be the booty call or the other girl.

Sherrice still believed in finding her Prince Charming. She wanted someone to sweep her off her feet and take her away from all the madness of the ghetto that she lived in. Was it so wrong to want a better life? She knew it was a long shot, but she was determined to find him.

For now, she would have to get her hustle on. After a few days of rest and getting her head together she would go down to the strip club where Lashay worked at. Her half of the bills still needed to get paid. She gulped down the rest of the beer left in the bottle and laid her head down on her pillow. Everything was going to be alright. Soon she was fast asleep dreaming of better days ahead.

David Givens

4

Ray Ray took the crack pipe away from his mouth and exhaled. He was so high he couldn't even move if he wanted to. He tossed the pipe on his coffee table and stared at his television in a daze. *"SportsCenter"* was on, but he really wasn't paying any attention. His mind was stuck on autopilot.

Life was good for him at the moment. He had a nice crib and a decent car. He was also down with one of the most respected crews in the city. To top it all off, he was cousins with Terry Law—one of the most feared men in the city. It wouldn't be long before he moved up the ladder and became a lieutenant. At least, that is what he fantasized about.

In reality, Ray Ray was a full blown crack addict. On the outside it looked like he had his shit together, however he was slowly digging himself a hole that he couldn't get out of. He found himself smoking up more and more of the product he was supposed to be selling. Fucking with the Sandman's money was a good way to become a ghost, but he wasn't sweating it though. He knew his cousin wouldn't let him go out like that. Family always stuck together.

Just then there was a pounding on Ray Ray's door. He moved his head a little, but he made no attempt to get up. Whoever it was would just have to come back. He wasn't about to ruin his high trying to talk to anyone at the moment. Then he heard a familiar voice cutting through the fog in his mind.

"Ray Ray, open the damn door. I need to hollar at you."

For a moment Ray Ray was confused. Maybe he was too high because he thought he heard his cousin at the door. Normally, Terry never stopped by his house. They always conducted business in the streets. He was going to have to cut down on his smoking. It was making him too paranoid.

"Ray Ray, open the fucking door. I know you're in there."

Now he knew for sure that it was Terry. Suddenly, he was very sober and alert. He jumped off the couch knocking over his coffee table in the process.

David Givens

Something had to be wrong for Terry to be at his house. It didn't take a rocket scientist to know that it was about the money he had fucked up.

Ray Ray looked frantically around for his Glock. The pounding on the door was growing steadily louder. He knew that in his neighborhood his neighbors wouldn't even bother to call the police. It wasn't worth the hassle. *Now where is that gun?*

He spotted it on his kitchen counter two seconds after the front door flew off its hinges. Everything happened in slow motion after that. Terry came through the door with his .45 blazing. Ray Ray ran for his kitchen as hollow point bullets rained down around him. He caught one to the left shoulder that spun him sideways. He regained his balance and kept running. To hell with the gun. It was about survival now.

He changed his course from the counter to the back door. There was no time to open it so he jumped though the giant window above his sink. He fell into his backyard in a shower of glass. Shards of glass impaled his body all over, but he couldn't stop. He rolled painfully to his feet and kept it moving.

The night air was cool on his skin as he ran down the back alley behind his house. The loose gravel caused him to lose his footing and fall into a row of garbage cans. He lay there dazed for a moment taking

David Givens

in short, raspy breaths. He knew his body was in a bad way, but the drugs in his system helped to fight off the pain.

Suddenly, he became aware that he was alone. There were no sounds to indicate that someone was chasing him. Maybe Terry was just trying to scare him? Yeah, that's what it was. It was a warning to tell him to stop fucking up. He laughed a crazy laugh at the thought.

Headlights appeared at the other end of the alley. Maybe he could flag down whoever it was so he could get to the hospital. The main thing was that he was still alive. Then he heard the engine gun and the vehicle raced toward him. Maybe it wasn't his lucky day after all.

Ray Ray tried to get to his feet, but it was no use. His legs snapped likes twigs as a large SUV rolled over them. He made a loud choking noise as he proceeded to scream and vomit at the same time. Pain washed over him in waves.

Terry got out of the SUV and walked over to where Ray Ray lay, struggling to breathe. He kicked him viciously to the side of head causing him to roll over onto his back. Terry stood back and admired his handiwork for a moment. Times like this made him feel truly alive.

David Givens

"Come on Terry, don't kill me, we fam. I'll get you the money!" Ray Ray pleaded with every once of strength he had left.

Terry knelt down and grabbed the broken man roughly by the sides of his face. "You knew the rules. You fuck with the Sandman's money then you bleed. Have the balls to die like a man." He spit in Ray Ray's face and walked back to the SUV.

Ray Ray stared up into the night sky mesmerized by the beauty of the faraway stars. He sent up a silent prayer to God hoping that he would have mercy upon him. That hope was dashed when Terry came back with a red gas can. The liquid burned his eyes and stung his many wounds. He knew Terry was going to kill him now, but he wished he just would have shot him and got it over with.

Ray Ray painfully rolled back over and tried in vain to drag himself away with his arms. He yelled for help, but he knew it would never come. Terry stood over him and pulled a blunt and a book of matches out of his pockets. He calmly struck a match and lit his blunt. After a few puffs he dropped the still lit match onto Ray Ray's back.

Terry was forced to take a few steps back as the flames engulfed his cousin. Ray Ray started to scream and twist around like a wild animal on the ground.

David Givens

After about a minute his voice died away and his body ceased to move. The flames continued to cook his corpse for another six minutes.

Terry stood in the shadows watching until the last flame disappeared. A sadistic smile played at the corners of his mouth. For some reason he really got off on killing people. It was like the ultimate high to him. He was almost sad that Ray Ray didn't last longer.

Finally, he snapped out of his trance and jumped into his SUV. His tires sent up a shower of gravel as he peeled off into the night looking through his cell phone for his latest booty call.

* * * *

Across town, on the upper west side, Darrell was pulling into his large three car garage. He parked his Lexus truck in between his Mercedes S550 and his Infiniti truck. All three vehicles were black like the color of his heart. He keyed in his security code on the wall-mounted keypad and walked into the lower level of his beautiful home.

The huge two-story house filled him with pride every time he walked in. He had just recently purchased the five bedroom, three bathroom home a few months ago. Not bad for a twenty-two-year-old black male with just a high school education. His footsteps echoed on the expensive marble floor of his kitchen as he walked through it. He removed his shoes before walking on the plush white carpet in his spacious living room.

His journey lead him up a winding staircase and down a long hallway on the second level. Finally he reached the master bedroom located at the end of the hall. He stripped down to his silk boxers and walked into the master bathroom that adjoined his bedroom. Soon steam appeared as hot water began to fill up the huge Jacuzzi tub located in the middle of the room.

Darrell then walked back to the mini bar located in his bedroom. Usually, his nightcap consisted of two shots of Hennessy. Tonight he filled up a medium sized glass with the golden amber liquid. There was a lot on his mind. Since the tub was going to take awhile to fill he put on a robe and walked down the hallway to his study.

The overhead lights came on automatically and dimmed to a low purple haze when he entered the room. He pushed a button on the wall and the blinds at the other end of the room slid away to reveal a huge picture window. The view of the city lights at night was both peaceful and amazing. He walked over to the window and gazed down upon the city. This was his city. This was Waterloo.

Waterloo was a small city fast on its way to becoming a large city. It was located in the Northeastern part of Iowa. Hustlers and businessmen on both coasts would smirk at Darrell when he told them where he was from. It never bothered him though. They could sleep on the Midwest while he stacked his paper to the sky.

Not too many people knew that Waterloo was smack dab in the middle of the Midwest drug game. Its two major highways made it possible to be in Minneapolis, Omaha, St. Louis, Kansas City, Chicago or Milwaukee in a matter of a few hours. This made the small city the ideal meeting place for a lot of the heavy hitters in the Midwest. Many deals were handled behind the scenes. Whoever controlled Waterloo stood to be a very powerful man in the game.

That's all that motivated Darrell at the moment. Sure he had money, expensive cars and women—however, he craved power. That was the missing piece in his jigsaw puzzle. To get that power he was going to have to go to war. He had spilled blood before to gain his position in the city, but this was going to be different.

There were a few other crews in the city that rivaled his own when it came to sheer brute force. The City View Clique, Crazy White Boys and Vatos Locos were the main threats. The City View Clique was a group of

David Givens

brothers who operated out of City View, a small gated subdivision located on the outskirts of the east side. They sold weed, coke and dabbled in prostitution. They usually bought their cocaine from the GMC, but Darrell had recently heard that they were going behind his back and trying to get a cheaper price from some out-of-town connects. That was reason enough alone to check them.

The Crazy White Boys were a crazy group of skin-head wannabes disguised as trailer park trash. They lived on a huge farm complex outside of the city and exclusively sold Meth—the new crack. Meth was fast becoming one of the most popular drugs of choice in the Midwest. It was three times more addictive than crack and could be made cheaper. No one cared that it was dangerous to make and had toxic side effects. It was a goldmine and the Crazy White Boys were raking in the dough. Darrell figured it was time some brothers got in on the action.

The Vatos Locos were a gang made up of Mexican immigrants who operated in the downtown area. They sold crack, weed, angel dust and ecstasy. They didn't buy their cocaine from the GMC, but Darrell wasn't tripping. He didn't really have a problem with them. The downtown area was full of cops at most times so he never operated there. The Vatos could have that part of the city as far as he was concerned.

So that left the City View Clique and the Crazy White Boys to be dealt with. He would also have to take out the L-Block Boys before they became too big of a problem. Hopefully, Loco and Jay could find out who they were connected to so he could squash future problems before they had a chance to surface. His plan was going to be difficult to accomplish, but it was doable.

The only snag would be the reaction of the Minister. The Minister ran a cult in the city disguised as a religious group. They were modeled after the Nation of Islam except that the followers worshiped him instead of Allah. He was deeply involved in politics and sat on the board of many prominent organizations. However, behind the scenes the Minister kept all the gangs and crews in check. Everyone had to break him off a piece of the pie. In exchange, he made sure that the cops and the district attorney looked the other way in most cases.

The Minister didn't really care who was on top in the dope game as long as he got his share. However, he didn't like a lot of trouble stirred up in his city either. Darrell didn't know how he would react to the bold move he was about to make. He didn't really want to piss him off, but he was ready for that, too.

He gulped down the rest of the Hennessy and closed

his blinds. The strong liquid warmed his insides as he proceeded back to his bathroom. He shed his robe and boxers and slid into the Jacuzzi. The hot, swirling water relaxed the taut muscles in his back. He pushed a button on the side of the Jacuzzi and soft jazz music filled the room.

In the months to come he was sure that he would finally realize his dream of taking over the city. The only question was, how much of the city would be left?

5

Detective Malik Thomas pulled up to a large crowd surrounding a modest house on Beech Street. He parked his unmarked sedan under a shade tree and rubbed his temples. The lingering effects of a hangover caused his brow to furrow. *It's a fucking circus out here,* he thought as put on his shades and stepped out of his car.

Waterloo didn't have many murders every year, so when one occurred it seemed like everyone overreacted and fell over themselves trying to figure out what happened. This case was no different. It was barely six in the morning and the street was already filled with nosey neighbors, television crews and dozens of plainclothes officers. A few reporters had already broken past the yellow tape and were being chased down by

          David Givens

officers.

Malik shook his head and fished in his pocket for a crumpled Newport. He lit it and ran his fingers through his kinky afro. It was time to start the show. He pushed his way through the crowd and past annoying reporters looking for answers. A few officers nodded at him as he made his way to the front of the house.

He noticed the front door had been kicked in. *This should be interesting.* When he walked inside he noticed the disarray in the house. A coffee table was pushed over and the walls were riddled with large bullet holes. The house was crowded with officers and forensic specialists. The place was a mad house. Malik dropped his spent Newport on the carpet and ground it out with the heel of his loafer.

"Could you please not do that, Detective?" asked one of the crime lab guys nearest to him.

Malik ignored him and walked over to the wall to examine the bullet holes. He determined they were caused by a large caliber gun. His first guess was a .45, but he would have to see the lab report to be sure. The kitchen was his next stop. He spotted a Glock sitting on the counter. It would be dusted for fingerprints later and run through a ballistics report to see if it was connected to any other unsolved crimes.

The back window caught his attention. Only a few

shards of glass remained within the pane. Some of them were covered in blood. He walked over to the window and peered through into the backyard. Glass and blood littered the grass below. He even saw what resembled a human ear lying amid the mess.

Malik closed his eyes and shut out the surrounding noise. He could see how the episode played out in his mind. The victim was sitting down watching television when the perp knocked on the door. He probably realized he was in trouble way too late. The overturned table and the untouched gun testified to that. The window was the quickest option for escape.

Malik opened his eyes and returned to the present. He opened the back door and walked out into the backyard. It was full of more lab guys and plainclothes officers. There were way too many people floating around contaminating his crime scene. On top of that the wet dew in the grass was seeping in through his cheap loafers, making his socks a soggy mess.

He followed a trail of blood out into the back alley. The alley was really just a small path made of gravel barely big enough to accommodate the large garbage trucks that ran through it once a week. There was a crowd of officers and a crime lab photographer in the alley surrounding a beautiful woman who was down on her knees studying what appeared to be a pile of

David Givens

black rubbish.

Malik sucked his stomach in as he got closer. He still had bulging biceps and wide shoulders from his athletic past. However, years of eating doughnuts and pizza had made him a little soft around the middle. He never really cared about his appearance that much, but she was working the case.

The she was Loretta Gibson. She was the best forensic investigator in the state and the subject of Malik's many wet dreams. Malik noticed that all the officers standing around her were rookies trying to sneak a peek at her beautiful ass that was up in the air at the moment. He quickly dismissed them and the photographer when he got close enough.

Loretta nodded her approval at him and continued to study the pile of rubbish on the ground. Upon closer inspection, Malik realized he was looking at the charred remains of a body. It made him crave another Newport in the worst way. Maybe that made him an uncaring bastard. At least that is what his two ex-wives liked to call him.

He stood for a moment and watched Loretta do her thing. She was a thick chocolate sister with a cute British accent and sexy bedroom eyes which she hid behind tinted glasses perched on her nose. Her hair was twisted into small dreads that hung down to her shoulders. Finally, she paused in her examination to scratch her ear.

"So what do you have for me?" asked Malik.

"The house was rented by one Raymond Law. It's safe to say that this is his body, but I won't be sure until I can check dental records. Apparently he was surprised by his attacker and jumped out the back window. Not before he sustained a gunshot wound to the shoulder. He fell into the garbage cans over there. Then his legs were severely fractured by being run over by a large vehicle. Then at some point he was doused with gasoline and set on fire. I put his time of death at around 12:45 a.m."

"Sounds like he pissed someone off really bad," said Malik as he scanned the alley for anything that stood out. Most likely any evidence would have been trampled on already by the overzealous officers on the scene.

Loretta gathered up her tools into a small back bag and moved out of the way as the coroner appeared to take the body away. Malik watched her dust off her jeans and adjust her glasses. He liked the way her jeans hugged her ample hips and superb backside. His growing erection caused him to turn his back to her.

"Could you have your people forward the forensics report to my desk as soon as it's done?" he asked.

David Givens

"Of course. My people are almost done with the house and the backyard. The report should be on your desk early tomorrow morning."

"By the way, are you free for dinner this weekend?" Malik asked as he turned to look at her sideways.

"Are you hitting on me at a crime scene, Detective?" Loretta cocked one eyebrow at him and placed her free hand on her hip.

"I didn't think our friend Raymond would mind," Malik said with a sly grin.

"I've heard of your rep with the ladies, Detective, and frankly I'm not impressed. I like to keep my personal life and my professional life on two separate planes." Loretta shook her head and walked off. She yelled back at Malik as she left, "By the way, I could still see your erection, pig."

At least she didn't say no, so I still have a chance. Malik let his belly bulge back out after she left. He searched his mind for any references of Raymond Law. Then the realization hit him like a ton of bricks. Raymond Law, a.k.a. Ray Ray, was the cousin of Terry Law.

Terry Law and his partner, Darrell Jenkins, had been a thorn in his side for far too long. Every time he was close to busting Terry, Darrell would come through with his high priced lawyers and get him off. They had even sued the police force for harassment after the last time and won. If Malik wasn't the best homicide detective on the force he would have been fired or demoted.

He knew no one would have the balls to kill Terry's cousin. That would mean a death sentence for the person and their whole family. Somehow Terry had to have been involved. It wasn't beneath him to kill someone in his family. Malik had seen enough of Terry's handiwork to know that he was one sick motherfucker.

A bad feeling settled in the pit of Malik's stomach. He knew if the GMC was involved then more killings were on the horizon. Two summers ago they had left a bloody path of unsolved murders in their wake on their rise to dominance in the streets. The city couldn't handle another one of those summers. This time Malik was going to get those bastards. They were going down once and for all.

David Givens

6

Darrell threw his newspaper down in disgust. Ray Ray's murder had made the front page and he wasn't happy about it. Terry tended to go over the top sometimes. A simple bullet to the head would have worked, but Terry had to go and set a motherfucker on fire. Who the hell barbeques their own cousin anyway?

On top of that, Detective Thomas had been assigned to the case. Darrell hated him with a passion. Detective Thomas was a former crooked cop that had once been on Big Rome's payroll. When Darrell took over Big Rome's spot, Detective Thomas showed up looking for a job. Darrell had laughed in his face and sent him on his way. There were two things in the game that he couldn't stand—a snitch-ass nigga and the fucking cops.

Since then, Detective Thomas had tried to make it hard on the GMC. Every time there was a murder, most of the crew was rounded up and interrogated for hours. Detective Thomas especially had it in for Terry. There was no love lost between the two since Terry had fucked the detective's younger sister over and left her a cracked out fiend. Darrell couldn't begin to count how many times he was in court last year using his lawyers to get Terry off on one of his many murder or drug beefs.

That was another reason why Terry wasn't really an equal partner. Darrell loved him like a brother, but he was too much of a loose cannon. He couldn't have someone like that in a leadership position. He'd worked way too hard to get where he was to have it all torn down because his boy was a psychotic killer with a short fuse. However, when it was time to get into some shit, Terry was the best guy to have on your side.

Darrell leaned back into his plush leather chair and let his mind wander back to a night two years ago. His mind was still messed up from catching his girl with Big Rome earlier in the day. Word on the street was that there was a hefty price tag on his head. He wasn't worried though. At that point in time he didn't care if he lived or not.

He was in a small bar downtown working on his

David Givens

fourth Hennessy and Coke. Most people saw the menacing look on the big man's face and left him alone. He was caught up in a whirlwind of anger and sadness that had him on edge. Keke had been his ride or die chick and Big Rome had been like an older brother to him. Now they had both betrayed him and played him like a punk. He didn't like that feeling one bit.

Darrell barely noticed the four young thugs who came swaggering into the bar like they owned the place. A lot of the other patrons did and they hurried up and made it out one of the nearest exits. The four young brothers stopped in front of Darrell's table. He finished his drink and slammed the glass down on the table with his left hand.

"Yo, nigga, you the Sandman?" asked the one in front. He was obviously the leader of the group. His eyes were glassy and his lips were pulled back into a sneer.

Darrell looked the baby-faced killers up and down. They couldn't have been more than sixteen or seventeen. They had their arms folded wearing mean scowls on their faces. He could tell they were strapped by the bulges under their shirts. He laughed at them because they were amateurs. He hoped they would see the death in his eyes and leave. Too bad they had other plans.

David Givens

"You think this is a game, nigga?" said the young wannabe killer. He reached under his shirt for his heat in one swift motion.

He never made it though. Darrell blew his intestines out his back with two shots from the Desert Eagle he had palmed under the table in his right hand. He pushed his table over then and caught the second thug with a shot to the head. His brains sprayed all over the bar. By this time the other two punks had recovered and pulled their guns.

Darrell fell to the floor as a shot grazed his shoulder. He rolled over and shot the nearest punk in the knee. He fell to the ground in agony. Darrell silenced him with a shot that tore out his throat. The last one tried to run. He received two shots to his back that sent him flying into an old jukebox in the corner. The jukebox came on and started playing "*A Change Is Gonna Come*" by Sam Cooke.

Darrell got to his feet and staggered to the bar. He peeled off a wad of bills and placed them on the bar. Then he was gone out into the night. The wound on his shoulder was more of a scratch, but it was bleeding heavily. He pulled into the nearest gas station so he could use the bathroom. While he was cleaning his wound his cell rang.

"What's up, Terry."

"I took care of that problem for you," Terry said on the other end.

"What are you talking about?"

"That nigga, Big Rome, is no more."

"How did that happen?" By now he had gotten a handle on the bleeding and was wrapping gauze around his shoulder.

"I went up the hospital to check out the scene. The pig that was supposed to be guarding his room was down the hallway talking to a little shortie and his boys were in the waiting room playing spades. I slipped in and put a pillow over that nigga's face. He woke up and tried to fight, but it was a done deal. I slipped back out and that shit was a wrap. You know I had to get that nigga for doing you foul and shit. Ain't nobody putting a price on my nigga's head."

"So no one saw you?"

"Man, I was in and out that bitch quick. Plus, I had on some scrubs and a mask that I had borrowed from a supply closet."

"That's straight. Good looking out my nigga. I'm about to go back to the hotel to rest. Some young niggas tried to get at me tonight."

"What, you alright? Tell me where you at so I can bring the pain. I'm ready to paint the town red my nigga. Them cats will be laid out by the morning."

"Naw, it's cool. They already a memory. I got grazed, but it's nothing major. I shouldn't have to worry no more since Big Rome is gone. Just meet me at the spot tomorrow. We gonna have to get a new crew together cause cats are going to be coming for Big Rome's spot. The streets are going to get ugly in the next couple of weeks."

"That's what I'm talking about. Finally, we get to lay some niggas to rest. I've been itching to try out my new Uzis. I'll hit you up tomorrow then. I'm gone, one."

Darrell shook his head at the memory. The following months after that night had been bloody. A lot of young soldiers in the game had their wigs split. The media had called it the worst murder spree in Waterloo history. The feds were even called in, but no one was talking. Over time the killings stopped and the buzz died down. Out of the ashes rose the GMC and it had been on and cracking ever since.

Now Darrell was sitting in his office that was located in the back of his recording studio. The profitable little studio was just another legitimate front to launder the mass amounts of drug money his crew was raking in. He also owned two gas stations, a restaurant and a car wash. On the outside he looked and played the part of a legit, taxpaying businessman. Other people knew him as the ruthless leader of a drug organization that

David Givens

was terrorizing the community. Both roles suited him well.

Darrell sat up in his chair and rubbed his temples. He could feel a headache coming on. Stress always caused him to get migraines. He popped a few aspirins and grabbed the phone on his desk. The line rang three times before Terry picked up.

"Whats good?" asked Terry.

"You tell me. I'm looking at the paper and it's not pretty."

"Shit gets out of hand sometimes. I just go with the flow."

Darrell's anger almost bubbled to the surface, but he held it in check. "Meet me at the gym later. We have to discuss a few things."

"That's cool with me. See you there, one."

Darrell put the receiver down and sighed. Terry was getting to be a little erratic lately. He loved his boy, but he needed his head to be on straight. There was a war brewing and he needed his top soldier to be on point when the shit hit the fan.

He left his office and walked down the hallway in between his two recording booths. The first one on the left was full of some grimey young cats that were members of the GMC. Tone, Chopper and Greg made up a group called the Young Riders. Their sound was a mixture of Dipset and Wu-Tang. They had built up a loyal following in the 'Loo and were now looking to break into the industry. Darrell thought they had a good chance. Plus, since he was their manager, he stood to make a nice chunk of change if they succeeded.

He didn't bother to check in on them though. He already knew they were doing their thing. Besides, he was on a mission. The aspirin wasn't doing a thing for his headache, but he had another type of stress reliever in the building. He walked through the next door and sat down next to Ray, one of his sound engineers. Ray was busy adjusting various knobs and buttons on the huge mixing board in front of him.

A big-boned, light-skinned female sat in the recording booth singing. Her hair was dyed platinum blond and she was wearing a skimpy outfit that appeared to be two sizes too small for her frame. Her average face was covered in too much make up and her large lips were coated in bright red lipstick. Every time it appeared that she was hitting a note, Ray scrunched up his face and adjusted another button. Since the booth was soundproof, Darrell was spared the sound of her voice. Ray on the other hand was wearing headphones that piped her voice directly into his ears.

Latoya thought she was one of the greatest singers to ever grace the planet earth. In her mind she was on

David Givens

par with Mariah Carey and Whitney Houston, before Bobby Brown. However, she was really tone deaf and had the range and sound of a bullfrog. Darrell knew she couldn't sing worth a lick, but he kept her around for her other talents.

Darrell waved through the glass and she stopped singing. Ray let out a sigh of relief. Latoya started smiling and came out of the booth. She hugged Darrell and made sure her huge breasts rubbed across his chest.

"Did you hear me getting down in there? I swear I was laying it down better than Ciara," Latoya bragged as she did a little dance.

Both men noticed the way her huge ass and titties jiggled while she did her little two step. "I'll hear you on the playback. Right now I need to talk to you in my office," said Darrell.

"Okay, Daddy."

Latoya turned and walked out into the hallway. Darrell admired the way her ass bounced when she walked. He could feel an erection coming on. When they got back to his office he closed and locked his door. Latoya was already down on her knees in front of the couch he had in the corner.

"Come here and let me relieve your stress, Big Daddy," Latoya said as she licked her lips.

Darrell sat down and unbuckled his pants. The

David Givens

young singer quickly stripped off her shirt and had his dick in her mouth before he could blink. He could already feel the stress leaving his body. Latoya made loud slurping sounds as she went to work. She gagged a few times, but handled him like a pro. Darrell soon had one of his huge hands palming the back of her head.

He fucked her mouth like a pussy for a few minutes before he started to feel an explosion coming on. Latoya could feel him tightening up and took his dick out of her mouth just in time. Darrell came all over her huge titties and slumped back into the couch. His headache was gone and a huge smile was plastered across his face.

Latoya got up and went to the bathroom to clean up. She returned with a warm wash cloth to clean up Darrell. When she was done she went back the bathroom to return the wash cloth and to put her shirt back on. Darrell was already up, standing by the door.

"Did you like that, Daddy?" she asked as she gave him another hug.

"Of course, I always do. Now get back out there and lay down those vocals so you can become the next big thing." Darrell playfully slapped her on the ass as she exited the room. He knew she would never be a star, but in exchange for free studio time she gave him some

David Givens

bomb-ass head that always seemed to take his headaches away. Besides, he didn't have to listen to her. However, he did make a mental note to increase Ray's pay.

Darrell walked swiftly to his desk and pulled a .38 from his drawer. He whirled toward his window, but no one was there. A minute ago he thought he saw a shadow cross by out the corner of his eye. He proceeded to the window and looked out. The alley behind his studio was empty. Maybe the head was so good that he was seeing things now? He chuckled to himself and tucked the .38 in the small of his back. A minute later he was locking up his office and leaving.

* * * *

In the shadows hidden behind a large dumpster sat a stranger. The stranger's heart was pumping wildly. The person waited for a few minutes before sneaking out of the alley.

7

Sherrice sat in the passenger seat inside Lashay's '04 Honda Civic. She had only been unemployed for one day, but now she was riding down to the strip club to see if she could get a job with her friend. There was just no way she was going to sit around broke. So many thoughts went through her mind as she stared out the window. Her stomach was tied up in knots.

"Don't worry, girl, you gonna knock 'em dead. Yo sexy ass will probably pull in almost as much dough as I do," said Lashay as she placed a hand on Sherrice's knee.

"I don't know about all that. I just want to make my share of the rent and be able to get a few things like a new car," said Sherrice as she brushed Lashay's hand away.

Sherrice had always known Lashay was bisexual and didn't have a problem with it. She had never hit on her before or even acted like she was interested—until now. Ever since Lashay had found out Sherrice was coming to the club with her she had started getting touchy feely. Sherrice was strickly dickly and hoped she wouldn't have to whip her friend's ass. It would put a damper on their living arrangements. Plus, home girl had always been a good friend.

Finally, they pulled up in front of an ordinary building that sat a mile back from the highway. The unlit neon sign read "Charlie's Place." The modest-looking strip club had become one of the best after-party spots in the city over the last five years. All the major ballers and hustlers in the city frequented the spot on the regular.

Both beautiful women got out of the car and walked through the humid, unpaved parking lot past the huge Suge Knight-looking bouncer and into the club. The smell of weed, sweat and pussy filled their nostrils as they navigated around the tables in the dimly lit club. Sherrice's eyes watered from all the cigarette and weed smoke in the air. Some nappy headed girl with little breasts and dimples in her huge ass was on the stage grooving to an R. Kelly song. Sherrice couldn't tell if the girl was doing the robot or having a seizure.

"All the weak-ass bitches work the morning shift," said Lashay nodding toward the girl on the stage. "They put fine-ass bitches like us on the stage at night when the big spenders come out."

Finally, they made it to a little office in the back. Lashay knocked on the door and it was opened by another huge bouncer. Behind a dented up metal desk sat a fat black woman in her late thirties. She sported a crew cut shaved close on the sides and had a scar that ran from the left side of her face underneath her eye down to her double chins. People said Charlie got the scar from fighting with a man when he walked in on her and his wife in the bedroom. The man ended up dead, but his death was ruled an accident. Apparently he fell on his own knife.

"So, Lashay, this is the friend you been telling me about? I have to admit she is fine," said Charlie as she came from around her desk and stood before the two women. "Very exotic looking. Now let's see what you're working with."

"What's that supposed to mean?" Sherrice asked. She looked from Lashay back to Charlie.

"I see you're a funny one, too. It means get naked, ho. I can't hire you if I don't know what I'm getting in the bargain," laughed Charlie. Lashay and the bouncer joined in on the laughter.

David Givens

Sherrice was very nervous now. She almost cursed them all out and ran for the door. However, she needed the money in the worst kind of way. Slowly, she started to shed her clothing until she stood before everyone in a matching purple bra and panty set. She looked down at the floor and blinked back her tears.

"Damn, now that's what I'm talking about," said Charlie as she licked her lips. The big woman circled Sherrice and let out a long whistle. "Now let's see them tits."

Sherrice looked up and saw everyone in the room staring at her with hungry eyes. Her hands shook as she undid her bra and let it drop to the floor. The room got so quiet you could almost hear a pin drop. The bouncer didn't even try to hide the huge erection growing in his pants. For a few seconds no one spoke. To Sherrice it seemed like an eternity.

Finally, Charlie snapped out of her trance and spoke. "Are they real?" she asked, never taking her eyes off Sherrice's chest.

"Bitch, I'm all natural," snapped Sherrice. She may have been nervous, but once again her mouth wasn't.

"Oh yeah I like you," laughed Charlie. "You start tomorrow as our main attraction. The house gets forty percent of what you make. Your stage name is Carmel Delight."

David Givens

"Hey, I'm the main attraction," whined Lashay from the corner.

"No baby, you were the main attraction. I'll give you a little bonus for bringing your friend in though."

Lashay frowned up her face and folded her arms across her chest. She was pissed and it showed. Sherrice quickly put her clothes on and followed her friend back out into the club. They entered a hallway that led to a large dressing room in the back. It was mostly empty since the club wasn't busy at the time. Two skinny-ass white girls sat chatting in the corner smoking cigarettes. Lashay led Sherrice over to a small locker on the other side of the room.

"This is where you will keep your outfits and shit. I suggest you bring a lock back with you tomorrow because hoes do be stealing shit up in here." Lashay paused for a moment and admired herself in a giant mirror that ran the full length of the opposite wall. "I can't believe that dyke-ass bitch gave you my spot," she mumbled as she adjusted her blouse to show off more of her ample cleavage.

"I can tell her I don't want to be the main attraction. I'm just here to work like everyone else." Sherrice really didn't want to start off on the wrong foot.

"Don't even trip, baby girl. Just remember that Charlie always gets what she wants. She is probably just trying to test me by doing some bogus shit. Everyone knows no one can drop it like it's hot better than me," said Lashay as she dropped down to the floor and came back up with her ass clapping.

Sherrice just shook her head at her friend and gave her a high five. They both fell out laughing. Soon they were back outside the club and in Lashay's car driving away. Sherrice was once again staring out the window trying to collect her thoughts. She just hoped in her heart that she was doing the right thing and that everything would turn out okay.

* * * *

Darrell was in the back of Gold's Gym getting his sweat on. He was currently doing dumbbell curls with a set of 65s. His already massive biceps were pumped up to the max. A grunt escaped his lips, but it wasn't from the stress of the weights. Terry was late and Darrell hated to be kept waiting.

He looked at his watch for the fifth time and proceeded to pump out two more reps for each arm. Then it was on to the barbell curl. Darrell slid one hundred pounds onto the bar to warm up with. He curled it for ten easy reps. By the time he reached two hundred pounds he had worked up a good sweat.

Terry chose this time to make his entrance. He came in wearing an all black velour jogging suit with black stunner shades on. His new platinum grill sparkled as he smiled and talked on his cell phone. He put his cell phone away as he stopped and chatted to a few young sisters over by the water fountain. Then he swaggered over to where Darrell was.

"You're late. Let's hit the bench press," said Darrell as he walked over to the weight bench. There was no use arguing with Terry about his tardiness; Darrell had figured that out a long time ago.

Darrell loaded the bar up with 175 lbs. for Terry to warm up with. He spotted for him as he pumped out eight reps. Then he had Terry load the bar up with 315 lbs for him. He squeezed out ten reps quite easily. The friends went back and forth until Terry maxed out at 250 lbs and Darrell maxed out at 585 lbs.

"So what's really good?" asked Terry as the friends sat in the locker room drinking Gatorade after their workout.

Darrell made sure that they were alone before he spoke. "What was up with torching your cousin? You could have just made him disappear. Detective Thomas will be sniffing around for sure now."

"Let that motherfucker sniff around. The police ain't trying to fuck with us ever since that lawsuit. However, that nigga Ray Ray had it coming. I'll bet niggas will think again before they fuck up the money."

David Givens

"That's not the point. I just don't think we need the added attention right now."

"Since when did you give a fuck about the way I handle my business, Sandman?" asked Terry as he got in Darrell's face.

"Calm your ass down and get out of my face before I forget you're my boy."

Terry never backed down from no one, but he wasn't stupid either. He and Darrell may have been equals when it came to gunplay, but in a fist fight he would be the loser. There would be nothing to gain by catching an ass whipping. Besides, Darrell was the only real friend that he trusted out in the streets. He sat down and patiently waited for him to go on.

"This is real talk my nigga. In a few weeks the GMC is going to be taking over all this shit. I'm not content with just having a piece of the pie. We taking the whole thing. You feel me?"

"That's what I'm talking about. There's always more money to be made," said Terry. His eyes glazed over for a few seconds as he thought about all the killing he was going to do.

"Just lay low for awhile. I'm meeting with Carlos in a couple of days to finalize some plans. Then it's on and popping."

"I can do that. Just keep me in the loop. Now what

about that Kanye West concert this weekend?"

"I already spoke to his people and hooked up the VIP treatment for all the crew. It's gonna be off the chain," Darrell said. He had known Kanye back when he was just a struggling producer trying to get someone to listen to his beats. They still stayed in touch over the years.

"That's all I needed to hear then. I'm about to go down to Burger King and eat. I'll check you later, one." He gave Darrell some dap and left.

Darrell sat in the locker room and stared at the wall. His mind was heavy and he didn't like the feeling. He wasn't worried about the upcoming war anymore, but something else was nagging at him. It was just below the surface; however he couldn't put his finger on it.

Maybe spending time with his son would help. He phoned Keke and told her to have his son ready to go in an hour. She tried to chat with him, but he hung up on her. There was nothing they needed to talk about unless it concerned his son. Finally, he left the gym and headed home to jump into the shower.

David Givens

8

Detective Thomas sat at his desk eating a barbequed chicken sandwich and drinking an orange soda. He was going over the forensic report on the Raymond Law case. So far he was getting nowhere. No one saw anything and no evidence was left at the scene to implicate Terry Law in the death of his cousin. He didn't know why he bothered sometimes.

His contacts on the street had informed him that it was business as usual for the GMC. However, what concerned him was the fact that no one had seen Darrell or Terry on the block since the killing. Something major was going down and he wanted to be there when it happened. He just knew that he was getting close to his chance of nailing those punks. They were going to suffer big time when he brought them

David Givens

down.

Detective Thomas' sister had been a lovely young girl when she ran into Terry Law. She was a straight A student and lettered in basketball. It was a case of a good girl being attracted to a bad boy. Malik and his parents had warned her that she was making a bad decision, but she wouldn't listen. She was blinded by love.

Malik let his sister make up her own mind and to this day he regretted it. Over time she became thinner and started acting strange. Every now and then she would show up with bruises and lie about how she got them. Malik confronted Terry once, but he was out-numbered and out gunned. Terry laughed in his face and it took everything he had in him not to pull out his gun and go out in a blaze of glory.

Then came the day when he found his sister float-ing in the bathtub with her wrists slit. He rushed her to the hospital in the nick of time and she lived. However, she was never the same again. Apparently, she had been heartbroken when she walked in on Terry fucking another girl. Now his sister was a ghost of her former self. She stayed in and out of rehab and suffered from depression.

From then on Malik had tried to make Terry's life a living hell. He kept arresting him time and time again

David Givens

even if he didn't have any evidence, hoping something would stick. However, he always got off thanks to the fucking Sandman and his lawyers. That muscle bound thug pretending to be a businessman really rubbed Malik the wrong way.

Malik hadn't always been a good cop. A couple of years ago he used to take bribes from Big Rome. In exchange he would tell him inside information on raids and investigations. It was a sweet deal for a while. The extra money came in handy after his second ex-wife tried to bleed him dry during their divorce. Then Big Rome had to up and get himself killed.

That wasn't even the worst part. When Malik tried to approach Darrell with the same business arrangement he was rudely turned away. The arrogant punk had actually laughed at him and said he was a disgrace! Like being a drug dealer was an honest profession. Now Malik's expensive lifestyle had eaten up his little stash and he was living check to check again. Yeah, those punks were going to pay big time. They just didn't know it yet.

"Hey, Detective, did you hear what I was saying to you?" asked a voice behind him.

Detective Thomas snapped out of his trance and noticed that he had crushed his half-eaten sandwich in his fist. He dropped the squishy mess on his desk and swiveled around in his chair. A young patrol cop named Jim Williams was standing before him. Malik had always liked him and thought he had a bright future on the force.

"I'm sorry, I most have been daydreaming," said Detective Thomas as he used a napkin to clean his hand off.

"The Chief wants to see you right away in his office."

Detective Thomas nodded at the young officer and swept the remains of his lunch into the waste basket by his desk. He produced a pink bottle of antacid from his drawer and guzzled it down before getting out of his chair. Talking to the chief always had a way of upsetting his stomach. He just hoped he didn't get yelled at too much this time. If it wasn't one thing it was another.

Michael Kincaid had been the police chief in Waterloo for the last ten years. During this time period more African Americans had been arrested than in the last fifty years before he arrived on the scene. He always claimed that he wasn't racist, but the patrol cars visible in the black neighborhoods had doubled since he had taken over. Currently, the NAACP and the Civil Rights Commission were breathing down his neck.

Detective Thomas stood before the chubby asshole

and waited patiently for him to get off the phone. Chief Kincaid knew the detective was waiting, but decided to take his sweet time talking dirty to his mistress on the other end. He never really cared for the black detective anyway. If he had his way all the ethnic officers on the force would be stuck working traffic and patrolling high school hallways. However, he did like the idea of using a nigger to catch niggers. The irony of the situation made him smile as he hung up the phone.

"So what leads do you have on the Raymond Law case?" asked the Chief as he lit up a cigar that was lying in the ashtray on his desk.

Detective Thomas didn't really want to say what he was about to say, but it had to come out. "I don't have any concrete leads at the moment. However, I do think Terry Law was somehow involved."

"Don't you even say that fucking name around here," said the chief as he slammed his fist down on the desk.

"Sir, if you would let me explain."

"No! Let me explain something to you. Leave that man alone. The last time you harassed him the station had to settle a huge lawsuit out of court. There would-n't have been a basis for the lawsuit if you didn't have a long track record of arresting him on bogus charges. The only reason you still have a badge is because that's the only blemish on your otherwise impeccable record. If it was up to me you would be bagging groceries at the local mini mart."

Detective Thomas winced at the mention of the lawsuit. It hadn't been his finest moment. His obsession and quest for vengeance against Terry Law had almost cost him his job. He would just have to be more careful in the future.

"Sir, that's all that I have to go on right now."

"Well hit the streets then. Somebody has to know something. Let me tell you this one time—if you do go after Terry Law again you better have something concrete or else you'll find yourself out of a job. Do I make myself clear?"

"Yes, sir," replied Detective Thomas as he turned and exited the office. He hated the chief with a passion and he was sure the feeling was mutual. It didn't matter at that moment though. Terry or Darrell were bound to slip up soon and he would be there to put them away. Then the chief's job would be his for the taking. The thought made him smile as he made his way out to the parking lot. His future was looking very bright indeed.

* * * *

Sherrice sat in front of her locker in the back of the strip club trying to overcome the butterflies she felt in

David Givens

her stomach. She pulled her beautiful hair back into a ponytail and surveyed the room. It was crowded with half-dressed women who were either naturally sexy or artificially enhanced to look sexier than what they were. A few of them looked her up and down with looks of disgust while others licked their lips and nodded at her.

A group of three tall Amazon looking bitches started to walk toward her until Lashay popped up by her side. Before Sherrice could protest Lashay had grabbed her by the back of the head and planted a passionate kiss on her lips. Her butterflies were now replaced by surprise and anger. She was about to kick some ass when she noticed the group of women nod at Lashay and fall back.

"What the fuck was that about?" she asked.

"That was just Stacy and her crew. They be on all the new bitches. I just kissed you to make them think you were with me so they wouldn't fuck with you."

"Well you could have warned me ahead of time. You know I don't play that shit," said Sherrice as she began to undress.

"I wish you did," Lashay mumbled under her breath as she secretly admired her friend's body.

Sherrice stripped down to a blue thong with a matching bikini top. Then she pulled a white blouse and a black skirt out of the duffle bag she had brought along with her. The blouse was of a see-through material and the skirt barely covered the cheeks of her ass. A pair of nerdy glasses and some silk stockings completed the outfit. She admired herself in the mirror for a moment and was amazed by the raw sex appeal that oozed from her appearance.

"Damn, you are one sexy motherfucker," a slender chocolate chick sporting dreads said from the other side of the room. Lashay shot her a look that made the girl look away.

On the outside Sherrice looked sexy and confident, but on the inside she was bugging out. *What the fuck am I doing here?* she thought to herself. There was just no way she was going out on the stage sober tonight. She needed a drink and she needed it now. Lashay tapped her on the shoulder and handed her a flask as if she had read her mind.

"Here, take a few swallows of this. It's Patrón mixed with lime juice. Most of the girls here go on stage high or tipsy. It helps get you through the night."

Sherrice hurriedly took the flask and took a long drink. Her face scrunched up from the taste. She wasn't really into anything harder than beer or a Smirnoff, but tonight was an exception. The liquor warmed her up and mellowed her out a little bit. She took two more sips then passed it back to her friend.

"Yo, Sexual Chocolate, you on," called a voice from the door.

Lashay got up and motioned for Sherrice to follow. They walked from the locker room to the backstage area in silence. "Okay girlfriend, just watch me from here and I'll show you how it's done. Time to take these niggas' money."

Lashay stalked out to the center of the stage as the lights dimmed and everything got quiet. She wore a black leather outfit that looked like the one Halle Berry wore in *"Catwoman."* Suddenly, *"Leather So Soft"* by Lil Wayne and Birdman started playing. Lashay looked up and started to contort her body to the music. Her flexibility was on full display as she dropped down into a split while keeping her ass clapping at the same time. Then she rolled onto all fours and crawled across the stage. When she proceeded to stand on her head while alternating between scissor kicking and clapping her ass, the crowd went wild.

Sherrice could only stare on in amazement. The liquor had her buzzed and her friend's exotic display had her slightly turned on—not to the point where she was thinking about switching teams, but maybe a little experimentation couldn't hurt. She shook her head to clear the crazy thought from her mind. The freaky

David Givens

atmosphere was getting to her and she didn't like it one bit. Damn, she needed to get laid soon.

She looked on as Lashay worked her way from one side of the stage to the next. Men of all ages and colors slapped her on her ass and put money in her leather garters. Those who couldn't get close enough threw cash onto the stage. Finally, her set was over and she collected her money and left the stage.

"There's nothing to it, baby girl. You see how I was killing those niggas? They couldn't get enough of my chocolate. I'm about to go work the room for private dances in the back. They should call you on in a minute. Just go with the flow and remember I'm out in the crowd and I got your back." Lashay stuffed her money into one of her boots and took off.

Sherrice took slow breaths and hoped no one noticed her shaking hands. How could she go on stage after Lashay's performance? She wasn't as confident or as seductive as Lashay. There was no way she could compete with the moves her friend had done. Suddenly, she heard her stage name being called. She hurried out onto the stage and hoped she didn't break an ankle in the five inch heels she was wearing.

The place got unusually quiet as she stood waiting for her music to cue up. There were hardly any background murmurs or even sounds of people moving

David Givens

around. Sherrice opened her eyes and saw almost everyone in the place had their eyes glued to the stage. Finally, *"I Wanna Fuck You"* by Snoop Dogg started bumping through the overhead speakers.

Sherrice started moving her body to the rhythm. At first her movements were a little stiff, but as the song went on she loosened up a bit. Before long she had shed her blouse and skirt and was walking around the stage like she owned it. There was so much money in her garters it felt like her legs were chaffing. Since she was the main attraction her time on stage was longer.

When *"Go Getta"* by Young Jeezy came on, she was in a zone. Before long she was twirling around the pole in the center of the stage upside down. In the middle of the song she shed her bikini top. There was damn near a riot as men pushed to the front of the stage to get a closer look. They weren't used to seeing such a fine specimen of woman in a dive like Charlie's. Security even had to put hands on a few drunken customers who wanted to climb up on stage.

When her set was over Sherrice grabbed up her out-fit and the piles of money on the stage. She rushed back to the now empty locker room to count how much she had made. After she reached the two thousand dol-lar mark, her eyes got blurry. It was more money than she had ever held at any one time. The dancing part

David Givens

wasn't that bad either. She was beginning to wonder why she was ever afraid to come here in the first place.

"You were wonderful tonight. I've never seen the customers go that crazy," said Charlie as she walked in with a bouncer and a strange man Sherrice had never seen before. The man was dressed in a ridiculous pink and gray pin-striped suit with a matching pink chinchilla on. He held a mahogany cane in his right hand and a pink bowler hat was cocked to the side on his head.

"This is Too Sweet and he is one of your biggest admirers," said Charlie as the man came forth and kissed the back of Sherrice's hand. "He would like to spend some time with you."

Sherrice didn't know what Charlie meant by the comment, but she didn't like the look on Too Sweet's face. He looked like a hungry cat waiting to pounce on a helpless canary. She shuddered and backed away a little. The whole situation had trouble written all over it.

"Don't be like that, baby. I just want to get to know you a little better. You should be happy a pimp like me even took the time out of his busy schedule to bless you with my presence."

"Excuse me, but I don't roll like that, partner. I'm just here to dance and that's it," said Sherrice as she

David Givens

stood up. At five-foot-ten she towered over the short pimp.

"Bitch, you better recognize a real pimp when you see one. Now why don't we go back into one of the back rooms and get to know each other better?" Too Sweet asked as he grabbed Sherrice by the elbow.

He never saw the punch coming. Sherrice nailed him with an overhand left that sent the short pimp staggering back. His hat fell off and landed on the floor. He grabbed his mouth and appeared to go crazy when he noticed his lip was busted.

"Bitch, I'll kill you!" Too Sweet screamed as he pulled out a switchblade and lunged at Sherrice.

The bouncer caught him before he could get to Sherrice and ripped the knife from his grasp. He then proceeded to push the enraged pimp from the locker room area. Sherrice let out a sigh of relief and relaxed. That's when Charlie hit her in the stomach. She fell to her knees gasping for air.

"You're new so I'll let you slide this time," said Charlie as she squatted down by Sherrice. "I own your little sexy ass now, so you'll entertain whomever I tell you to entertain. And don't even think about not show-ing up for work tomorrow. I'll find you anywhere you go. Trust me, you don't want to make me look for you. Get with the program and we all make money. Fuck

David Givens

with me and you'll be sorry. You understand?"

"Yes," Sherrice said with tears in her eyes.

"That's more like it. I'll just take this," Charlie said as she took all the money that Sherrice had just made on stage. "You cost me money by dissing a valued customer, so I'll take this to make up for it. Now get your ass out there and do some private dances."

Sherrice sat down on the cold concrete floor as Charlie left. *What the hell just happened?* One moment she was happy and paid—now she was pissed and broke again. This was some bullshit. Now she knew for sure it was a bad idea to come down here. How in the hell was she going to get herself out of this crazy mess?

David Givens

9

Thursday morning came about too quickly for Darrell's taste. He rolled over in his huge California king bed and knocked his alarm clock off the nearby dresser. It landed on the floor, but still continued to ring like mad. The sound was like a jackhammer to his ears.

Finally, he got up and turned the stupid device off. Then he grabbed his remote from under the covers and turned on his sixty-inch plasma screen television. He changed the channel to ESPN so he could catch the highlights of the NBA playoffs from last night. Hopefully, the Jazz beat the Spurs. He had a lot of money riding on the game.

Suddenly his son burst through his bedroom door and jumped into the bed with him. They playfully tussled for a moment before he tickled the toddler into submission. It was nice having his son around the house. They had spent the last two days together going to parks, catching movies and spending a mountain of money at the toy store.

Darrell loved spoiling his son. It probably had something to do with making up for the relationship he never had with his father. Sammy Jenkins had been a hustler and a rolling stone. The man never settled down in one place too long. Darrell could count on one hand how many times he had seen his father.

He never wanted to do that to his son. Even though Keke had shattered all hopes of them being a family he was going to be there for his son and make sure he grew up to be a better man than he was. His son would never have to worry about a damn thing as long as there was still breath in his body. Their bond was undeniable to any and all who saw them together.

"Daddy, do I have to go home today?" asked the cute little boy. He loved spending time with his father. His mother was mean and barely paid him any attention.

Darrell wished his son could stay for a few more days, but he had a lot of business to take care of. "Yes you do, but I'll make it up to you, little man. I promise."

"I love you daddy," said Darrell Jr. as he hugged his father.

Darrell had to blink back tears as he hugged his son

David Givens

back. The little guy always had a way of getting past his hard exterior. "I love you too, son."

Two hours later, Darrell sat at the back table in his restaurant eating a stack of buckwheat pancakes with scrambled eggs while drinking decaf. He was dressed in a pin-striped charcoal Armani suit with a blood red tie. An expensive Satellite laptop computer sat on the table to his left. When he was done with his meal he pushed his plate to the side and pulled the laptop closer.

He skillfully entered in a few encrypted passwords and logged into a secure chat room online. Now he just had to wait for a few minutes until the appointed time. While he waited a short Latina came out and cleared his dishes away. He winked at her and she blushed. She refilled his coffee quickly and left him alone to work.

At the appointed time a message popped up on the screen:

SAVIOR: *2 your mid*

Savior was the handle used by Carlos Diaz. His message translated to "Tomorrow at your place, noon." He was a big time Colombian cocaine supplier among other things. Darrell had started doing business with him last summer after the supplier he was using could no longer meet his demands in a timely manner. Carlos had been the man above the man he was using and was impressed by the amounts Darrell was able to move in Waterloo and in its surrounding areas.

Darrell quickly typed back a response:

DISCIPLE: *O c thn. Oer biz cus so.*

His reply meant, "Okay, see you then. I have other business to discuss also." Darrell cut his connection and closed the laptop. Everything was running smoothly so far. Tomorrow he would meet with Carlos like he did every month like clockwork. Only this time he would be ordering more than just good cocaine. The anticipation of the impending meeting made him smile briefly.

The sound of the front door opening made him look up in time to see Terry, Jay and Loco entering the restaurant. Each man wore a black outfit. Black was the color that represented the GMC. They all gave Darrell some dap and sat down at the table with him. The short Latina appeared again and took their orders. She screwed her face up at Terry before she left.

"What have I told you about fucking the waitresses here?" asked Darrell as he looked in Terry's direction.

"I can't help it if light-skinned negros are making a comeback. Besides she only sucked my dick so that doesn't count."

Each man cracked up with laughter at Terry's wild remark. They were still laughing and talking shit amongst each other when the waitress came back with their food. Terry smiled at her and she stuck up her middle finger at him. This caused another round of laughter between the friends.

When they were alone again Darrell decided to get down to business. "So what did you guys find out about them L-Block niggas?"

Jay was a tall Creole brother with a lazy eye and mad basketball skills. He was well liked and respected in the hood for his slick moves on the black top. This made it easy for him to keep his ears to the streets. "Word is that J-Ice is related to the Minister in some way. He doesn't have his full backing, but he is fam," said the lanky ballplayer as he bit into a sausage.

Darrell nodded his head as he digested the information. It had caught him off guard and that wasn't a good thing. J-Ice and his young crew could be a problem in the future. However, if he was related to the Minister it wouldn't be a good move to knock him off just yet.

"We should just put two slugs in the back of his head and call it a day anyway. The Minister got to be slipping if he letting that young fool run around all reckless and shit. If he want it after that then he can get it too." Loco lived up to his nickname in more ways than one. The jet black, bald head killer was almost as bloodthirsty as Terry. He was down to bang with anyone at anytime.

"Let's just chill on that for now. If J-Ice brings the drama then we will take him out. I don't care who he is connected to. Everyone bleeds the same." The subject was done as far as Darrell was concerned.

"Yo, we got to go down to Charlie's tonight. I heard there is a new girl there that is off the chain." Terry was a regular down at the strip club. He loved tossing money in the air to make it rain. The look on the broke niggas' faces was priceless when he came through big balling out of control.

"The last time you said that we came down there and saw this buck-toothed, cockeyed ho with more stretch marks than Star Jones," laughed Jay.

"Fuck you, nigga. I was drunk and high at the time."

"When are you not?"

The men went back and forth cracking on each other for a few more minutes. Even Darrell found himself enjoying the conversation. This was what it was all about. There was a time when his crew was just a bunch of snot nosed young boys running errands for the old heads while dreaming of getting real money. Now each man at the table was earning over six figures and having the time of their lives.

"Okay, you cats knock it off. If I laugh anymore my breakfast will come back up. Let's hit Charlie's tonight though. You better not have us coming down there to

David Givens

see no chickenhead ho, either." Darrell hadn't been out in awhile. He figured he could relax tonight and maybe even go home with a new breezy. It would also be a good distraction for him since he had a lot on his mind lately.

Soon all the food was eaten and the friends parted ways. Terry went to check on the auto body shop he owned while Jay and Loco hit the streets to make sure the operation was running smoothly. Darrell grabbed his laptop and headed out to his Benz. He needed to stop by his two gas stations before he got his car detailed later at his car wash. The overpriced accountant he paid to keep his fraudulent books was doing a great job, but he liked to stop in on his businesses personally every now and then to go over the data himself. No one ever stayed on top for long if they didn't know what was going on around them.

The stranger sat across the street on a park bench watching the restaurant. Oversized shades and a baseball cap pulled low concealed the person's identity. Little did Darrell know that a plan was in the works to destroy their little empire, and that one of their own was in on it.

10

Darrell pulled into the dusty parking lot of Charlie's Place a little after ten. He parked his Lexus truck close to the front door and hopped out. The parking lot was pretty packed and he nodded at a few people who waved at him. He looked dressed down in a plain white tee and blue jeans, however his jeans cost nine hundred dollars and the ice on his neck and wrist were at least worth seven times that amount. Some people who didn't know who he was thought he was an NFL star who just happened to be passing through town.

The bouncer quickly opened the door for him when he approached and stepped aside. If he would have searched Darrell he would have found a 9mm in the small of his back and a twenty-two in his ankle holster. The club was smoky and humid. Dancers were mingling with the crowd doing cheap lap dances and trying to get the ballers into the back rooms for the more lucrative private dances. Of course, if your money was right there would be more than just dancing going on in the back rooms.

Darrell proceeded to the VIP area where he found Terry, Loco and Jay posted up at a private booth enjoying themselves. Huge bottles of Grey Goose and Belvedere lined the table next to an exotic array of drugs. A few well-endowed strippers sat amongst the gangsters. Darrell sat down and quickly ordered a bottle of Patrón Burdeos from a sexy topless waitress nearby. He liked to keep his liquor dark.

"What's up my nigga?" Terry said as he gave Darrell some dap. "You see we got it crackin' already. Yo bitches, say hi to my boy." The three strippers at the table all said hi and waved with goofy smiles plastered on their faces. It was plain to see that they were all well on their way to being fucked up already.

Darrell gave his other boys some dap and grabbed one of the many blunts off the table. He lit it up and inhaled deeply. It was filled with some good purple haze that had him feeling mellow in a matter of minutes. The waitress came back shortly with his bottle. He knocked back two big gulps before giving her a twenty dollar tip and sending her on her way. Now he

David Givens

was ready to be entertained.

"When does this shortie you were talking about come on?"

"She gets on at midnight. I'm telling you I've only heard good shit about her."

"That's what's up then. You know I'm clowning you if she's whack though."

Darrell settled in and watched the scenery around him. The VIP was filled with dealers, hustlers, pimps and a few legit businessmen. He even saw a judge with his face buried in the bosom of a young Puerto Rican chick with a phat ass. The place was jumping, the music was booming and the vibe he was getting was good. Maybe he would have to look into opening up a strip club in the near future.

He excused himself from the table after an hour to use the restroom. While he waited in line he felt something brush up against his arm. He ignored it at first until it brushed up against his arm again. Standing next to him was Lashay Goodson. She had been rubbing her exposed breasts up against his arm to get his attention.

"What's up Sandman? I haven't seen you in here in awhile." Lashay had been walking through the crowd when she spotted him from across the room. She knew he was probably the biggest baller there tonight. She

David Givens

could practically smell the money on him. Now she had to figure out how she was going to go home with some of it.

"I've just been busy doing a little of this and a little of that. You know how it is." Darrell really didn't feel like talking to the golddigging ho. Her body was banging, but her rep was laughable in the hood. She was known for getting down and dirty for the cash. In fact, he had walked in on Terry and a few other guys in the crew running a train on her in the back of the recording studio a few weeks ago.

"So what's up with going into one of the back rooms with me later on?" Lashay stepped back to give him the full view of her assets. "I can make it worth your time." She touched the tip of her tongue to her nose at the end of the statement to let him know what was up.

Her little display didn't have the desired effect on Darrell. He was actually turned off by it. A few months ago he would have taken her to one of the back rooms, threw some cash in her face and fucked her until he felt he'd received his money's worth. Now he just felt embarrassed to even be standing by her. He was tired of women who always had their hand out like he was an ATM. If he wanted that he would have stayed with Keke.

"Naw, I'm straight. Terry is over in the VIP. You might want to hit him up." Darrell moved ahead in the line and turned his back on the experienced golddigger. She would be getting no cash from him tonight.

Lashay stood there stunned for a moment. She wasn't used to rejection. *This nigga must be gay,* she thought to herself. There was just no way a sane man would turn down what she had to offer. She flipped her hair in a dismissive manner and stomped off in search of another victim.

Darrell quickly used the restroom and made it back to the table just in time to see Terry partying hard. His boy had his head tilted back looking at the ceiling with a powdery white substance on his nose. One of the strippers was under the table giving him a blowjob. Darrell sat down and shook his head. Terry was just being himself. However, Darrell didn't know his boy was doing coke. He would definitely have to keep an eye on him.

Just then the lights dimmed low and a spotlight appeared on the center stage. Darrell sat up in his seat and took another sip of his Patrón. "Ladies and Gentlemen, Charlie's Place would like to introduce the main attraction for tonight. Give a nice round of applause for the one and only Carmel Delight." Loud applause erupted after the deejay's announcement.

David Givens

Apparently, the new dancer had already created a big buzz after only one night of dancing.

Darrell's whole world changed when the light-skinned beauty known as Carmel Delight walked onto the stage. It was like time slowed down and everyone else in the room had disappeared. She moved with a style and grace that was head and shoulders above any other woman in the place. Her body was like a moving work of art. If she wasn't perfect then she was damn near close to it.

He watched her dance to music he couldn't hear. His senses were so attuned to her that nothing else even registered to them. When their eyes met, a bolt of electricity shot through him from the top of his head to the soles of his feet. She paused for a split second before continuing her routine as if she had been hit with the same bolt. Her eyes seemed to hold all the answers to every question in the universe. He knew at that very moment that he had to have her no matter what.

"Yo, you alright Sandman?" Jay had noticed his boy was in la la land.

"Huh? Yeah I'm cool. Just have a lot on my mind."

"Looks like you have a stripper on your mind. Don't be turning into T-Pain on me," laughed Terry from across the table.

David Givens

"She is amazing though. Definitely a ten." Darrell was already thinking of ways to approach her.

"Man, her body is off the hook. I'd let her sit on my face," slurred Loco from his position. He was fucked up as usual.

"I told you guys you wouldn't be disappointed." Terry sat back with a smile on his face. He glanced at Darrell for a moment. His boy looked like he was in a trance while he stared at the stage. He'd never seen him like that before.

Darrell watched the angel before him finish her routine and exit the stage. His mouth had suddenly gone dry so he downed the rest of his bottle in one long gulp. It gave him an immediate buzz. He looked frantically through the crowd to see where she had gone. When he didn't spot her he stood up and left the table. His boys asked him where he was going, but their questions fell on deaf ears. He was a man on a mission.

Finally, he spotted her going toward the back of the club. The way she walked was poetry in motion. Her hips swayed back and forth like the rhythmic movements of ocean waves. He stalked her silently like a lion on the prowl. She entered the back hallway and was stopped by a man who looked vaguely familiar to him.

David Givens

He fell back a little to assess the situation. Something didn't seem right. It appeared that she was arguing with the man. Suddenly, the man slapped the dancer and pulled her into a room off to the side. That was all Darrell needed to see.

11

Up until that point, Sherrice had been having a decent day. She had put the whole situation with Charlie from the other day behind her. She didn't want to get down for the cash like Lashay, but she had little choice in the matter. There was money to be made and she was flat broke. It was all about survival of the fittest.

Her plan was to work a few months and save some money then she would disappear and leave this terrible place behind. The months ahead would be hard. She wasn't built to be a ho; it just wasn't in her nature. However, she would have to go through with the bullshit so she could make a fresh start somewhere else.

She was still mad at Lashay though. The heifer was supposed to be her girl, but she never warned her

David Givens

about how Charlie got down. In fact, she swore she saw the bitch smirk when she told her about what happened last night. Jealousy was a motherfucker.

By the time she arrived at the club earlier she had accepted her fate. After a few shots of Hpnotiq she was in the right mindset. The jealous looks from the other dancers didn't even faze her. She had a job to do and she damn well didn't have time for no drama.

Lashay tried to offer her a little coke, but she declined it. Drinking was one thing, but getting fucked up on anything stronger than weed was not her style. She got dressed and waited for her turn on the stage. There were no more butterflies in her stomach today. The thought of getting money and getting the hell out of this shit hole had her focused.

When the deejay announced her name she came out and did her thing. She had practiced all morning on her movements so she looked more polished. Everything was going smoothly until she saw him. The man in the VIP section stood out from everyone else. His mere presence radiated power and danger at the same time.

Their eyes locked and she momentarily lost herself in his dark, smoldering gaze. She paused for a split second then regrouped. No matter how fine he was she still had to finish her set and get that money.

David Givens

When the music stopped she gathered her money and left the stage. It was time to change into another outfit and work the floor. Hopefully, he would still be in the VIP when she came back out.

She was so lost in her thoughts that she didn't see Too Sweet pop up in front of her out of nowhere. He was dressed in a powder blue silk shirt with matching slacks. His hair was permed and pulled back into a ponytail. The sneer on his face revealed a mouth full of gold teeth. It also showed that his top lip was bruised and twice its normal size.

"What's up bitch? You thought you could just hit a pimp like Too Sweet and get away with it?"

"Whatever nigga, you got what you deserved. Now move around." Sherrice was not in the mood to be dealing with the short pimp. She glanced around to see if security was nearby.

"Don't bother looking for help. I paid the bouncer to take a long break. Me and you got some business to settle."

"I'm not going anywhere with your punk ass." Sherrice was beginning to get scared. She hoped he wouldn't try anything with a club full of people around.

In a flash, Too Sweet slapped the shit out of her. She saw bright lights and was slightly aware of someone grabbing her roughly by the neck and tossing her

David Givens

through a doorway. A couple of punches to her gut doubled her over. Then she was forced down to her knees. The sound of pants being unzipped could be heard. Too Sweet grabbed a handful of her hair and yanked her head back.

"You ain't so tough now are you, bitch? It's time to pay your dues." Too Sweet shoved his limp penis in her face. "Be a good girl and suck this dick or I'll cut your face up."

Sherrice thought about yelling for help, but realized no one would be able to hear her over the music. She was in no condition to fight back either. It looked like she was going to have to suck his nasty little dick and hope that he didn't kill her afterwards. There was no way out.

"Get the fuck off her," said a booming voice that suddenly entered the room. Sherrice's mystery man stood in the doorway looking like he was carved out of granite. His huge hands were clenched into bone smashing fists. The look in his eyes was purely murderous.

"Sandman...wh...wh...what the fuck are you doing in here? This doesn't concern you," said the small pimp. He was visibly shaken by the presence of the large man.

"I won't ask you again." The threat in his tone was

David Givens

unmistakable.

"Fuck you." Too Sweet wanted to at least retain a little of his manhood in front of the stripper.

The stranger rushed the little man and snatched him up with lightning speed. One moment he was in front of Sherrice, the next moment he was flying across the room headfirst into a wall. Too Sweet tried to struggle to his feet, but the stranger was already on him kicking away savagely at his prone body. After a few sharp kicks to the head he lay in a daze on the floor groaning. His face was bloody and unrecognizable.

The stranger stood over his victim breathing heavily while clenching and unclenching his fists. His eyes were wild with anger until they fell upon Sherrice. The anger turned to concern as he hurried toward her and helped her up off the floor. His touch was surprisingly gentle.

"Are you okay?" His voice was a smooth baritone. He told her his name was Darrell and he just happened to be passing by when he saw what happened.

Sherrice nodded and stumbled up against him. His strong arms embraced her and held her steady. They walked toward the doorway in silence. Suddenly, Charlie appeared in the doorway with two huge bouncers behind her.

"What the hell happened in here?"

David Givens

"Don't act stupid, Charlie. We both know you have cameras in this room. Now get out the way. The girl is coming with me." Darrell's hand slid behind his back and gripped his 9mm just in case Charlie's trained monkeys wanted to act up.

"Now why would I let you take my newest star? You may be one of the baddest motherfuckers in these streets, but in here we play by my rules." Charlie smiled wickedly. Normally she wouldn't fuck with someone with the Sandman's rep, but the coke in her system combined with the two big men beside her made her feel invincible.

"Bitch, the only rule that matters is never fuck with the GMC," said Terry as he came up behind Charlie with his .45 on display. Loco and Jay were close behind with their guns drawn also. "I hope you ain't fucking with my man here, or I'm gone have to put two hot ones in your ass."

Charlie whirled around with wide eyes when she saw the huge gun in her face. However, she was more scared of who was holding the gun. Getting the drop on the Sandman was one thing, but going against his crew was a good way to end up dead. Especially when the psychopath known as Terry Law was around.

"Everything is cool. I was just telling the Sandman to enjoy the rest of his evening." Charlie looked at her

David Givens

bouncers for help, but they were already on the ground with their hands up hoping they didn't get a bullet in between the eyes. They were smart enough to know what was up.

"I figured it was something like that. Sandman, grab your girl and let's ride. I was getting tired of this place anyway. The service sucks and the bitches ain't shit."

Darrell led Sherrice toward the door. As he passed Charlie he stopped to speak. "I want you gone in the morning. One of my men will stop by for you to sign over ownership. I don't ever want to see you in Waterloo again. Try me and they won't be able to find enough of your body to identify you."

Charlie knew how the GMC got down, so she knew his threat was good. She was going to miss her club, but it wasn't worth dying over. Maybe it was time for an early retirement anyway. There was a house by the lake in Toronto with her name on it. When the gangsters left she kicked the nearest bouncer in the back causing him to fall on his face. You could never find good help when you needed it.

Darrell got Sherrice outside and put her into his truck. He walked over to where Terry was posted up by his Land Rover. "I want you to come back when they close with a few boys and have her sign ownership over to you. Give her six hours to vacate the city. If she

David Givens

is even a second late in leaving the city limits then put a bullet in her head. I hate for anyone to think they can try me."

"That's cool; I always wanted to have a strip club. Now what's up with you and old girl up in the truck? I know you gone hit that. You went through too much trouble not to."

"Naw, it ain't even like that. I was just helping short-ie out. I'll take her home and whatever happens after that is anyone's guess." Darrell was really feeling the dancer, but he wasn't about to push up on her after the episode that transpired in the club.

"Shit, she fine as hell. I'd bang that back out and be snoring before the sun came up."

Darrell laughed with his guys for a moment. Terry was just being himself. He shook hands with his crew and then went back to his truck. Sherrice was inside shivering and looking out the window. Darrell took a blanket out of his backseat and wrapped her in it. He then started up the vehicle, turned up the heat and drove off into the night. Hopefully this was the start of something good.

David Givens

12

Sherrice still couldn't fully comprehend what all had happened. One moment she was on stage then the next she was being whisked out the club by the man from the VIP section. Now here she was sitting inside an expensive truck with a man she barely knew driving through the city. She glanced over at him to get a better look.

He was very handsome at first glance. His dark chocolate skin contrasted well with the crispy white T-shirt he was wearing. She noticed how his bicep bulged out of the shirt like a huge cannonball. His chest also stretched the limits of the fabric. *So I see he works out.* The jewelry on his neck, ears and wrists shined brightly in the dark. Apparently, he made a lot of money which was also a good thing.

David Givens

She flinched as the memories from what happened earlier came back to her. Too Sweet was going to pay for putting his nasty little dick in her face. There was no way she was going back to the club now. She would just have to find someplace else to work at.

So this is the Sandman. She had heard that name in the streets many times over the last few years. He was supposed to be a big time drug dealer and killer. No matter what he did for a living he was her hero now.

She settled back into the soft leather heated seat and relaxed. What a day it had been. All the excitement had her drowsy. She couldn't wait to get home and crawl into bed. Her face still hurt from the slap, but it didn't appear like there would be any swelling.

"Excuse me, but what is your name?" Darrell asked suddenly from driver's seat. He glanced over at her for a second. She was more beautiful up close.

"It's Sherrice. And don't think I'm going to sleep with you just because you saved me." She hadn't meant for that comment to slip out, but her mouth as always had a mind of its own.

Darrell chuckled to himself. He instantly liked her personality. She wasn't a pushover or fake with it. The kind of woman he could fall for. That is, if he was looking for a woman. At the moment he was enjoying the single life.

David Givens

"Well it's nice to meet you, Sherrice. I don't want to sleep with you—at least not yet. However, I'd be honored if you would go out with me sometime." Darrell smiled at her showing off his dimples.

"That sounds innocent enough. Besides, it's the least I could do since you kicked the shit out of that wannabe pimp for me." They both started laughing at her comment. It hurt her face to laugh, but she did it anyway.

"I have tickets to the Kanye West concert this weekend if you are interested."

"I'd love to go! I've never been to a concert before."

"Then it's a date. Now why don't you tell me where you live? I don't mind driving you around all night, but gas is high as a motherfucker." Darrell laughed again.

His laugh was both rich and deep. Sherrice really liked the way it sounded to her ears. She told him her address and they made a little more small talk. He was really starting to grow on her already. For some reason she felt comfortable around him.

They pulled up to her rundown apartment building after a few minutes. Sherrice was a little sad that her time with him was already over. He was intelligent, funny and full of class. This didn't go with the picture that the streets painted of him. Plus the man was fine with a capital F!

David Givens

Darrell looked around at her neighborhood and shook his head. A woman so beautiful didn't deserve to live in a place like this. She was a diamond in the rough. He could tell she was more than a pretty face also. She was easily the baddest chick in Waterloo. He had to have her.

"So are you going to give me your number or do you want me to throw rocks at every window until I find yours?" He was in a joking mood tonight, a mood he was rarely in.

Sherrice smiled and they exchanged numbers. He gave her his house, cell and business numbers. Apparently, he really wanted to keep in touch with her. She knew she had him then. Her hand paused on the door and she turned back to look at him.

They stared at each other in silence for a moment. Neither one wanted to speak for fear of ruining the moment. Darrell wondered what was making him act this way. He had been around many beautiful women before and none of them affected him this way.

"I guess you're not going back to the club anymore. In my opinion you were too beautiful to work there in the first place. So what are you going to do?"

"I don't really know at the moment. I was working at a restaurant before."

"How would you like to manage a restaurant?"

David Givens

Darrell had recently fired the manager at his soul food restaurant. He was managing it himself at the moment, but he was way too busy to focus on running the restaurant and manage his other commitments at the same time.

"I don't know the first thing about managing a restaurant."

"It's okay, I'll have someone teach you. I know you will do fine. Just say yes or I will bother you everyday until you do."

"Okay then. You are just too good to be true." Sherrice leaned toward him and gave him a hug. To Darrell's surprise she also gave him a quick kiss on the lips. The brief contact made his nature rise.

Then just like that she was gone out the truck and running up to the front of the apartment building with his blanket wrapped around her. She turned and waved before disappearing into the building. Darrell sat in his truck for a moment savoring the sweet scent her perfume left behind. He hoped he knew what he was doing. The last time he let a woman into his world he ended up heartbroken.

J-Ice sat in his Tahoe across the street in a liquor store parking lot. He was puffing on a blunt and drinking a forty. He saw Darrell pull off in his flashy truck.

David Givens

The envy in his heart made him screw up his face. He hated the fact that Darrell had everything he didn't. The motherfucker had more money, better looks and a better rep.

Now it appeared that he had the best looking girl in the city also. He still remembered how the bitch had shot him down earlier in the week. What made Darrell so special? He was a man just like him. J-Ice was being a hater, but he didn't care.

Maybe it was because was he sitting alone in his truck with no women in sight. His fat belly and nasty demeanor didn't exactly attract the ladies. Even the gold diggers wouldn't fuck with him unless they were behind in rent. He was just an asshole and everyone knew it.

He took a few more hits of his blunt and let his anger bubble to the surface. He was the nephew of the Minister, damn it! If anyone was supposed to be big balling and having all the ladies fall all over them it should have been him. Instead he ran a small crew of young, lazy-ass niggas.

He looked down on the block and saw that none of his soldiers were out making his money. It was a damn shame. He was going to have to find them and bust some ass. The motherfuckers had no concept of what it really meant to grind. The GMC was out at all times of the day and night making all the money while his crew played PlayStation 3 and chased after bitches.

He rolled down his window and threw the half-full forty out onto the pavement. Some lazy-ass niggas were about to be in for a pistol whipping. When he was done with them he would set his sights on the Sandman. The punk was sitting in the position that was rightfully his and he was coming to take it back.

* * * *

Sherrice entered her apartment and went straight to her room and turned on the television. She slipped out of her stripper outfit and walked across the hallway into the bathroom. A hot shower would help get the stink of the club off her. She slid under the water and let it scald her skin clean.

When she was done she wrapped a towel around herself and walked into the kitchen. There was a piece of chocolate cake in the fridge that was calling her name. She grabbed the cake and a fork then went back into her room. An old black and white romance movie was playing on her television. It held her attention for a few minutes.

Soon she was daydreaming about Darrell. He was a question mark surrounded by danger. Was he as bad as people said? What were his intentions for her? Many questions swirled around in her head as she fell asleep.

David Givens

She was awakened by the front door closing a few hours later. Her roommate stumbled past her door into the bathroom in a rush. She could hear Lashay vomiting on the other side of the door. The heifer was drunk as usual. There weren't many nights that Lashay didn't come in from the club drunk as hell.

When she was done she staggered into Sherrice's room. "What the fuck happened to you, bitch?"

"I got a ride. Sorry I didn't tell you, but everything was hectic at the time."

"You know Too Sweet got taken away in an ambulance. I heard you had a nigga jump him."

"Naw, it didn't even go down like that. That fool was trying to rape me and the Sandman came in and fucked him up."

"What would the Sandman be doing helping you?" Lashay was more than a little bit jealous now. That motherfucker had dissed her, but had gone to save her roommate. She wasn't even concerned that her roommate could have been harmed or killed. Her lack of concern didn't go unnoticed by Sherrice.

"I don't know, but I'm glad he did. He also gave me a ride home."

"Did you fuck him?"

"That's none of your business. If you must know, I didn't." Sherrice didn't like Lashay's tone or her line of questioning. She wished she would just take her drunk ass down the hallway to her room.

"That's too bad. I would have fucked that fine-ass nigga and got some cash out of him. You know he paid."

"That's not what life is all about, Lashay."

"Bitch please. We use these niggas or they use us. That's the way it is." Lashay was slurring heavily now. She fell against the wall, but stayed on her feet. "Speaking of niggas, you know that Terry Law had the nerve to come in at closing time to say he owned the club now?"

"That's a surprise."

"That's what I was saying. Charlie took off early and said she wasn't going to run the club anymore because she had a family emergency that would make her relocate out of town. That sounds fishy, but I'm not complaining. I don't mind working for Terry. You know he got a big dick. He can work that motherfucker, too." Lashay giggled and swayed to her left. Sherrice jumped up and caught her before she could fall to the floor.

"I'll get you to your bed," Sherrice said as she guided her friend out of her room and down the hallway. She helped her friend undress and tucked her in.

"You know you can join me. I've seen the way you look at me." That was another thing that Sherrice hated

David Givens

about Lashay when she was drunk. Her bisexual nature usually came to the surface in full force.

"Goodnight Lashay," said Sherrice as she closed her roommate's door.

All this drama in the household was going to have to stop. Sherrice couldn't handle it anymore. Lashay's behavior was getting old. She was going to take Darrell up on his offer of employment. Dating him wouldn't hurt either.

13

Darrell arrived at his soul food restaurant two hours before noon on Friday. He looked up and down the street to make sure some of his men were parked in cars stationed around the block and on both sides of the street. A few men were on his roof and on the surrounding roofs of other buildings. Everyone was strapped and ready for whatever. Security was always a major concern whenever Carlos Diaz came to town.

Carlos was the cousin of a Colombian politician who was endorsed by the United States. Since the U.S. supported his cousin, the government tended to look the other way while Carlos trafficked drugs into America. This didn't stop them from arresting some of his partners every now and then to make it look like they were doing their job. Darrell wasn't trying to become one of those examples.

Carlos ran a phoney import/export business out of Chicago. With the help of his cousin he was able to get his drugs sent through customs disguised as artwork and various other things without getting checked. His whole operation ran like clockwork down to even the smallest detail. His estimated net worth was somewhere around 300 to 500 million dollars. It was once said that he was responsible for one third of the cocaine coming into America.

He was the top dog in the Midwest. There was no one higher. That fact alone made him very paranoid. That's why he spoke in code over the computer and only met Darrell once a month for thirty minutes at a time. Most people never got to meet him in person so Darrell was always honored by the visits.

Darrell walked into his restaurant and greeted his men stationed inside. He made sure the restaurant was shut down for the day. Two men with assault rifles followed him to the specially built soundproof back room. The room was swept for listening devices while he watched. When he was sure that it was secure he had his men leave.

Carlos Diaz arrived at the Waterloo Airport in his private G5 jet twenty minutes before noon. He exited the jet with four armed bodyguards and jumped into a

waiting black Rolls-Royce Phantom. The car was bulletproof as well as bombproof. He had it shipped down
the day before. Two black Jeep Commanders filled with
armed bodyguards flanked the car in the front and
back. The whole caravan pulled up in front of Darrell's
restaurant five minutes before noon.

Carlos got out surrounded by his guards and
entered the restaurant. He left his men in the front
room while he walked into the back room alone.
Darrell stood up and embraced his friend when he
came in. Both men were decked out in dark linen outfits with Gucci loafers.

Carlos removed his Versace shades and sat down.
He was a tall, dark-skinned Colombian in his mid-for-
ties with wavy black hair and a thin mustache. "How
are you today, my friend?"

"As well as can be expected. How was your flight?"

"My new jet is wonderful. I may get another one.
You should really think about investing in one."

"I'll have to look into that. I don't think I'm that well
off just yet," laughed Darrell.

Darrell admired and respected Carlos immensely.
The man had the power, respect and wealth that he
was hungry for. Carlos, in turn, liked Darrell because of
his drive and determination at such a young age. He
reminded him of himself.

David Givens

"So is it the usual order this time?"

"I'll take forty this time."

Carlos looked up at the young hustler for a moment. Then a smile creased his normally serious face. Finally, the young man was getting ambitious. Darrell's small crew usually moved between fifteen to twenty kilos a month. Now he wanted to move up to forty kilos. This must mean he was making a serious power move.

"This is very good news, indeed. I take it business is going well then?"

"You know it. I'm thinking about expanding a little bit now."

"I wish you well on your endeavors then. Now about this other business."

Darrell produced a piece of paper and slid it across the table. Carlos read it twice then crumpled up the paper and set it on fire with a lighter he took from his breast pocket. He set the burning paper in a nearby ashtray. His face was grim with understanding. He nodded his head in agreement then switched subjects.

"The weather is getting nicer. Tell me, Darrell, have you ever been down to Colombia?"

"I haven't traveled in a while. Building an empire is time consuming." The last time Darrell had left the states was when he surprised Keke with a trip to Jamaica when he had made his first ten grand in the game. The memory brought a smile to his face.

"I would agree. My country is a beautiful place. I have a huge estate there. You should come down and visit me there sometime." Carlos looked at his platinum Rolex and rose to his feet. He always followed his schedule to the letter. "My, how the time flies. I must be going, my friend. Both of your deliveries will arrive at your warehouse on Monday. Wire the payment to the usual accounts." Carlos started to exit the room, but then he paused and turned around. "Be careful, my friend. Never make a major move without checking all the angles first. My father taught me that."

Darrell let the words soak in as the older man and his entourage left the building. That's why he respected Carlos. The man had class and wisdom beyond his years. That was also the reason why he never let Terry sit in on his meetings with him. Terry's arrogant swagger and ill manners would probably cause Carlos to stop visiting as well as embarrass the hell out of Darrell.

The small piece of paper in the ashtray was reduced to ash now. Darrell had written a list of guns, ammo and a few other things he would need on it. On Monday it would all be delivered along with forty kilos of pure Peruvian cocaine to a small warehouse outside of the city that he never visited before and couldn't be traced back in ownership to him. Life was good indeed.

Darrell walked back into the front room and dismissed most of his men so they could hit the streets. They weren't making any money if they were standing around doing security. He walked into the kitchen area and pulled out his cell phone. Terry picked up after one ring.

"What's up my nigga? Your meeting must be over already?"

"He just left. Everything is going according to plan."

"So when am I going to meet the head honcho? I be putting in serious work out in these streets."

"It's all good. He's just a little paranoid. You don't stay around as long as he has in the game if you're not. It took me awhile to meet him myself."

"I understand that, but just put a bug in his ear about me. I'm your man, right?"

"You my guy since forever. No doubt. I'll hollar at him about you, but I can't make any promises. Anyway I need you to do something for me."

"Drop it on me then."

"Contact all the lieutenants and have them meet us down at the spot on Monday night. It's time to let all plans be known."

"It's about time my nigga. Shit is about to pop off in this bitch. I'll get right on that. By the way, who are you bringing to the concert? I got this ill shortie that I pushed up on at the mall coming with me. She look like a black Barbie."

"I'm taking that stripper from last night with me."

"For real? I knew you were feeling her. She is mad fine though. Did you hit last night?"

"Naw, the timing was all wrong."

"There is never a wrong time for getting some ass."

"You know what I mean, nigga. I'll hit you up tomorrow."

"Alright then, one."

Darrell put his phone away and thought about calling Sherrice. He pushed the thought away as soon as he had it. If he called too soon it would look like he was sprung or feeling her. He didn't want her to get a big head. However, there was something he did want to do for her. He flipped his cell phone back open and made a few phone calls.

David Givens

14

Sherrice woke up early Saturday with a huge smile on her face. Tonight she would see Darrell again. The concert would be great, but she was really looking forward to being in the presence of the mysterious thug.

Yesterday had been one of the longest days of her life. She had lounged around the house all day staring at her cell phone wishing it would ring. There were the usual calls from old friends and bill collectors, but nothing from Darrell. It didn't surprise her though. Someone with his rep would be used to girls falling all over him. He would expect her to call.

She didn't want to appear like a sprung chicken-head so she didn't call him. Now the ball was in his court. He was taking her to the concert so he would have to call.

Sherrice stretched and got out of bed. She walked out into the hallway headed toward the kitchen. The sight of her tore up living room made her pause. Cans of beer and bottles of liquor were strewn about all over the place. Furniture was pushed over and clothing was scattered everywhere. A couple of used condoms lay on the floor. Sherrice could only shake her head. This shit was getting out of hand.

Lashay was passed out in the middle of the mess on the couch with no clothing on. A half naked white boy was laid out next to her snoring. He looked like a lawyer or a doctor type. Another white boy, who was probably his friend, lay on the floor drooling in his sleep. Sherrice scrunched up her nose and stepped over him into the kitchen.

Her roommate was really starting to disgust her. It was one thing to fuck for money, but she could at least have some respect for her and their apartment. She lived there too and didn't want to see that shit all the time. Seeing half-naked, out-of-shape white boys early in the morning wasn't how she wanted to start off her day.

Sherrice grabbed a skillet out the cabinet and some food out of the fridge. She went to work on preparing some breakfast while her nasty-ass roommate and her guests slept off last night's freaky adventure. The smell

David Givens

of the eggs, turkey bacon and toast made her stomach grumble. Apparently, the smell caught her roommate's attention too, because when she turned around, Lashay was standing in the doorway yawning and looking at her.

"You up early and shit. I guess when you don't work you have all types of energy."

"What the fuck is that supposed to mean? You know what happened at the club." Sherrice wasn't really in the mood to be arguing with Lashay. Especially with two strangers in the next room.

"I know you just sat around on your ass all day yesterday looking crazy waiting for that nigga to call you. The Sandman is a boss player. He is not thinking about you. Maybe if you would have fucked him he would have broke you off with some change so you would have your half of this month's rent."

"Whatever, bitch. For your information he offered me a job managing his restaurant. So I will have my half of the rent in time. I don't have to fuck for cash like you." Sherrice knew her roommate would be pissed at her last comment, but she didn't care. It was too early in the morning and the bitch was working her last nerve.

She looked up in time to see her roommate rushing at her. In a flash the shorter, thicker woman was on her flailing away and trying to grab her hair. Sherrice was too shocked to do anything at first. She hadn't expected the naked ho to start fighting with her. A slap to the jaw knocked her back into reality.

She grabbed a handful of Lashay's cheap weave and yanked it out. Then she backed up and punched her roommate in the eye. This caused the bitch to grab her eye and let out a war cry before she rushed Sherrice again. They fell into the counter and knocked over some dishes. Then they were on the floor rolling around pulling each other's hair and cursing. In midst of their struggle Sherrice's T-shirt was ripped open, exposing her breasts.

The sound of their front door opening and closing caused both women to stop fighting. They lay on the floor with their hair fucked up, panting like they just ran a race. When Sherrice finally got up she walked into the living room and saw that the white boys were gone. A noise outside made her run to the window.

She looked out and saw the white boys running down the street still half naked. One had knocked over a garbage can in his haste. They jumped into a Lincoln Navigator and peeled out of the parking lot across the street like the world was coming to an end. The whole scene was comical and made her laugh. She looked over at Lashay, who had joined her at the window, and she was laughing, too.

"I guess we scared the hell out of them. They probably never seen no shit like that before," said Sherrice as she wiped the tears from her eyes.

"They'll think twice about coming to the hood again. That's for sure. At least they left my money." Lashay walked over to the coffee table and picked up the four hundred dollars that was laying there. "I should have charged them extra while I was at it. Both of them couldn't fuck worth a damn."

"Listen, Lashay, I'm sorry for what I said. I've just been stressed lately."

"It's cool. I shouldn't have reacted like that anyway. I know what I do isn't what most people would consider right, but I'm just trying to survive the best way I know how."

"So are we straight now?"

"Yeah, you know you will always be my girl. I still can't believe you punched me in my eye like that though. Who do you think you are, Laila Ali?"

Both women started laughing again. Sherrice came over and hugged her friend. Their relationship may not have been the best, but they were each other's only family. When Sherrice tried to pull back, Lashay held on tighter. Then her hands began to explore Sherrice's body.

David Givens

"What the hell are you doing, Lashay?"

"Don't fight it, baby. We both know this is what you want." Lashay tried to kiss her friend.

"Okay, you need to back up off me." Sherrice pushed her friend away. "I know you are not trying to start another fight up in here already."

"Come on, stop bullshitting. I see the way you be looking at me. You walk around here all sexy and shit. Plus you never have a man. What do you want me to think?"

"Lashay, you are my girl and I love you, but I don't go that way. I don't date much because most of these niggas around here ain't shit and I don't want to put myself out there. I respect myself too much for that."

"Okay I understand, but if you ever want to cross over to the other side let me know." Lashay proceeded to do a sexy dance in the middle of the room. She cupped her right breast in her hand and licked the nipple.

"If you don't get your nasty ass out of here," laughed Sherrice as she threw a pillow at her naked friend.

An hour later both roommates had showered and put on sweats. Lashay had cleaned up the living room and now they were sitting in the kitchen eating the reheated remains of the breakfast Sherrice had started cooking earlier. Both women were deep into their own

David Givens

thoughts. Sherrice was thinking of Darrell and what she would wear to the concert while Lashay was silently fuming inside.

Lashay played the good role of being a friend on the outside, but she was really a selfish gold digger who only thought of herself. She was secretly jealous of Sherrice's good looks. Of course she was fine, too, but Sherrice had a natural beauty that she didn't even try to flaunt. The sister was damn near perfect and she didn't even know it.

Her looks weren't the only thing that bothered Lashay. It seemed like no matter what happened, Sherrice always managed to land on her feet. Poverty, living in the ghetto and not having a real family never broke her spirit like so many other girls in the hood. She always appeared to walk around with a halo on her head.

Sherrice was everything that Lashay was not and that was the real reason why she hated her. Looking at her everyday made Lashay feel more and more embarrassed by her lifestyle. Now this bitch might have landed one of biggest ballers in the city. Life just wasn't fair.

Lashay hoped Darrell was just messing with Sherrice's head. If he didn't call and take her to the concert then she would be crushed. Of course, good old Lashay would be there to pick up the pieces. Besides, if anyone deserved to be taken anywhere it was her.

Both women were surprised by the ringing of the doorbell. No one would be coming to visit them this early on a Saturday. Lashay hurried over to the kitchen counter and picked up a dime bag of weed she had laying there. It could be the police and she wasn't taking any chances. She ran down the hallway and stashed it in her room. Sherrice grabbed her mace out of her purse and cautiously approached the door.

"Who is it?" she asked as she looked out the peephole. There appeared to be a man in the hallway in a brown uniform holding a large box.

"It's UPS with a delivery."

Sherrice put her mace away and opened the door. The man handed her a clipboard and a pen. She looked at the name and realized the package was sent to her. That struck her as odd since she knew she didn't order anything. She quickly signed for it, grabbed the package and shut the door.

"Who is it from? Hurry up and open it," said Lashay coming from the hallway.

"It says it was sent from New York, but I don't know anyone from New York." Sherrice busied herself with tearing open the wrapping on the huge box.

When she got the box open she found three smaller boxes inside. The biggest one contained a short black

David Givens

Prada dress with spaghetti straps. Sherrice almost fainted when she saw it. The next box contained a matching black Prada purse. And the last box held a pair of three inch black Manolo heels. Amazingly, everything was in the proper size.

"Oh my God, girl! That stuff had to cost over ten grand at least. Who sent you that?" Lashay sounded happy for her girl, but inside she was pissed. She also knew who sent it and that made her even more pissed. In all of her golddigging days no man had ever spent that much money on her.

"It doesn't say who sent it." Sherrice had a pretty good idea who it was from though. Just then her cell phone rang. The number came up as private, but she answered anyway.

"Do you like what I got for you to wear tonight?" asked Darrell on the other end.

"Everything is beautiful. How did you know my sizes?"

"I have my sources." Darrell had actually called Lashay the day before for the info. The trick had the nerve to charge him, too. Hearing the excitement in Sherrice's voice was well worth the two hundred dollars he paid.

"This was so unexpected. Thank you so much. Wait a minute, how did you know I just received your gift?"

David Givens

"Why don't you look out your window?"

Sherrice quickly got up and ran to the living room window. She looked down into the parking lot and saw Darrell posted up outside sitting on the hood of a black Benz. He looked like a model in his tailor-made navy blue suit. He removed his shades and smiled up at her. She swore her heart almost melted when she saw his pearly whites.

"So are you going to come down here and see a brother or do I have to come up there and get you?"

"I'm not dressed right and my hair isn't done," Sherrice whined. Her hair was pulled back into a pony-tail and the sweats she had on were wrinkled.

"Woman, I don't think you could ever look bad. Now get down here and show me some love."

Sherrice hung up her phone and was running down the stairs almost before Darrell's last sentence was out of his mouth. She burst out of the apartment complex and ran straight toward the man of her dreams. Her plan had been to play it cool when she got downstairs, but all that flew out the window when she saw him standing there with his arms outstretched. She flew into his arms and to her own surprise she kissed him. They stood there for a full minute locked together in a passionate kiss.

"Damn girl, if I knew all it took was a dress I would

David Givens

have bought you the whole store," Darrell laughed as he stepped back.

"Oh you got jokes." Sherrice playfully hit him in the arm. "You still ain't getting any. I was just shocked that you would do something like this for me. You don't even know me like that. Hell, you might not even like me by the time the night is over."

"I'll take my chances. I'm a good judge of character and you seem like a person worth knowing."

"What are your real intentions, Darrell? When a man spends this type of money on a woman he usually wants something in return. I'm not for sale if that's what this is about." Sherrice put her hands on her hips and sucked her teeth to emphasize her point.

Darrell was amused by her sudden change in demeanor. She really was something special. He was going to enjoy cracking her shell and getting to know the real her. "I don't want anything from you, but your time. Now if you would go upstairs and get your friend I have a special morning planned out for the both of you."

"How do you know I didn't have plans? And what do you have in mind?" asked Sherrice. For the first time she noticed a black stretched limo parked behind Darrell's Benz. The uniformed driver stood off to the side at attention.

David Givens

"Stop playing hard to get and go get your friend. I'll fill you in when you get back down here."

Sherrice raced back up the stairs and into her apartment. She told Lashay what Darrell had said and both girls hurried into their rooms to put on something more flattering. Sherrice emerged five minutes later in a white blouse and blue jeans while Lashay opted for a black form-fitting jumpsuit that showed off her curves. They hurried back outside where Darrell was waiting, still smiling, looking at his watch.

"It took you ladies long enough."

"You can't rush perfection," said Lashay as she walked up and tripped on an imaginary rock. Darrell slid over and caught her in his arms easily. She made a big show of clutching onto his chest and arms. Sherrice could only roll her eyes at her friend's foolishness. *The nerve of that bitch.*

"I'm so clumsy. You are too strong. All these muscles just bulging out everywhere. You must work out a lot," Lashay said as she tried to look innocent.

"You should be more careful." Darrell knew what Lashay was up to and he wasn't playing that game. If she wasn't Sherrice's friend he wouldn't have anything to do with her. He placed her back on her feet and got back to business.

"I've arranged for you ladies to be driven downtown

to a spa I know and be given the full treatment—a facial, manicure, pedicure, skin exfoliation and a full body massage. Next, my driver will take you to the Brown Bottle for lunch and then it's on to the hairstylist in the afternoon. I would like you ladies to look your best for the concert tonight." Darrell didn't really want to take Lashay along, but that was part of the deal he had agreed to in order to get the information about Sherrice. This was one of the times he hated being a man of his word.

"This is really too much. I don't know what to say." Sherrice was outdone. No one had ever been this nice to her in her whole life.

"Just enjoy yourself. I'll be back later on to get you for the concert."

Sherrice ran up to Darrell again and gave him another hug and an even longer kiss. Then she hopped into the waiting limo with Lashay. She rolled down the tinted window and waved at Darrell as the limo pulled off.

Darrell stood in the parking lot watching the ladies leave. If Terry were there he would have smacked him upside his head and told him he was tricking off, especially since he hadn't even fucked the girl yet. Maybe he was tricking off just a tad bit, but what was the use in having money if he couldn't impress people with it? He

David Givens

had to admit it made him feel good to see Sherrice's eyes light up.

He didn't know where things were headed with Sherrice, but he sure as hell was going to enjoy the ride. It had been a long time since he had pursued a female. They usually came after him. He found the change of pace interesting. If she thought this was too much then she hadn't seen nothing yet. This was only the tip of the iceberg.

David Givens

15

Sherrice looked into the full length mirror in her room and realized for once just how beautiful she truly was. The treatment at the spa had her skin glowing and her dress clung to her body like an expensive second skin. Her long hair was swept up on her head. She had-n't worn it like that in a long time. The only things that bothered her were the small cubic zirconia earrings in her ears and the fake pearls around her neck. She wished she had some real jewelry to set the outfit off right.

Lashay stood in the doorway admiring her friend. She was full of envy, but she had to admit her girl looked stunning. Lashay was wearing a short fire-engine-red cocktail dress that barely covered her ass. If she bent over slightly everyone would be able to get a good look at her goods. Her hair was done in micro braids that came down a little past her shoulders with the help of weave. She had on a pair of red Jimmy Choo heels that were killing her feet, but if she landed a baller tonight it would be well worth the pain.

The sound of a horn outside made both women look out the window. The sight of a stretched black Chrysler 300C made their mouths hang open. Behind it were two stretched Hummers that were also black. The GMC was on the scene for sure.

When the women exited the building all Darrell could do was stare in awe at Sherrice. She was simply amazing. He loved the way her long athletic legs looked in the dress he bought. She must have been an angel in disguise. The driver opened the door and the ladies got in.

Sherrice scooted over next to Darrell while Lashay sat on the other side of her. There were three other couples in the car. Terry, Loco and Jay each had beautiful, well-dressed ladies with them. All three men couldn't keep their eyes off of Sherrice. That was until Darrell cleared his throat and glared at them. Lashay stifled a laugh while the other ladies gave Sherrice dirty looks. Her presence made them all feel a little insecure.

The caravan of vehicles pulled away from the curb and began the journey toward the UNI-Dome. The UNI-

David Givens

Dome was located in Cedar Falls, Waterloo's neighbor-
ing city. It was a large indoor stadium where the
University of Northern Iowa held its home football
games. Tonight it was the site for the Kanye West concert that had been sold out for three weeks. Kanye,
Common, John Legend, The Roots and Keyshia Cole
were supposed to perform. Darrell had hooked it up so
that his group, The Young Riders, got to open up the
show with one song.

Sherrice looked over and admired how handsome
Darrell looked in his black long sleeve shirt and slacks
by Roberto Cavalli. The man had a class and style that
set him apart from his thug friends. All the other men
in the car were decked out in black T-shirts or jerseys
with tilted baseball caps and tons of platinum and gold
jewelry on. They looked like rappers while Darrell
looked like a business tycoon.

"You look so beautiful tonight," Darrell whispered
into Sherrice's ear.

"Thank you."

"I have another surprise for you."

"I don't know if I can take anymore of your surprises. You've already done too much for me."

Darrell reached behind him and pulled out two jewelry boxes which he handed to Sherrice. Everyone
stopped their individual conversations and stared at

them wondering what was inside the boxes. Sherrice opened the first one and saw a small necklace made of white gold and glittering diamonds. The second box held a pair of two carat diamond earrings.

"They are so beautiful. I don't know what say," said Sherrice as Darrell took off her cheap jewelry and replaced it with the new stuff.

"Just say thank you."

Sherrice thanked Darrell with a passionate French kiss that had everyone in the car cheering—everyone except for Lashay. She remained silent and stared out the window. Her envy was getting the best of her and she didn't want it to show.

Terry sat toward the front of the vehicle with his arm around a chick whose name he couldn't remember. He rolled his eyes at his friend's display of affection. As far as he knew, Darrell hadn't fucked the ho yet. The man was tricking off and getting played big time in his eyes. However, Sherrice was one fine looking piece of ass. He hoped he would get a chance to hit it after Darrell got tired of her.

The caravan pulled up to the UNI-Dome at 6:15 p.m. The concert didn't start until seven, but the surrounding parking lots were already starting to fill up. The GMC had front door service so they didn't have to worry. Every crew member that rode along exited the

David Givens

vehicles dressed in all black. They fanned out around Darrell and the head lieutenants like a black cloud. Everyone outside stopped and stared like they were celebrities.

Sherrice had seen nothing like it before. She felt like a movie star as she held onto Darrell's arm. Some people were actually taking pictures and pointing. They were doing it big and she was enjoying every minute of it.

Security rushed them inside past the gawkers and haters stuck in line. They were lead past the many rows of auditorium style seats toward a special VIP area lined with comfortable couches set up near the stage. Before they could fully reach the area, a small group of young thugs popped up in their path.

Sherrice sucked her teeth when she realized it was J-Ice and his crew. They locked eyes and he blew a kiss at her. She returned the favor with her middle finger. Darrell and Terry stepped to the front of the group and had security stand down while they addressed J-Ice.

"What you want little nigga?" The bass in Darrell's voice sounded like thunder.

"I'm just trying to get to my seat and enjoy the show, playboy. I didn't even see you guys coming." J-Ice grinned and acted like he was seeing the huge entourage for the first time. "Damn, you players are doing it real big. When I grow up I want to be just like you." J-Ice laughed at his own weak joke and soon his crew joined in.

"Bitch-ass nigga, I'll lay you out right now!" Terry stepped toward the fat punk with his hand underneath his shirt. Darrell put his hand out and stopped him before he could reveal his gun and start blazing.

"That's right, you better put a leash on your dog."

"No, little man, you better put a muzzle on your fucking mouth. Your next words could be your last words. Now I suggest you clowns move around before they carry you out zipped up in bags." Darrell invaded J-Ice's space and stood toe-to-toe with the shorter man. He was almost a full foot taller than him.

J-Ice backed up and noticed for the first time the bulges underneath the GMC members' shirts. They were all strapped and ready to go. His small crew on the other hand had gotten patted down at the door like everyone else. From the looks of it, the security crews were also down with the GMC. With his crew outnumbered and outgunned, J-Ice had no choice but to back down.

"I'll see you around then, nigga." J-Ice tried to sound hard, but his voice cracked. He quickly stormed off with his crew close on his heels.

"You should've let me smoke him," said Terry at the

David Givens

retreating gang leader's back.

"In due time, my nigga, in due time."

Sherrice let out a sigh of relief. She was happy that her dream night didn't end in disaster before it even began. It was crazy how Darrell could shift from being a gentleman one moment then to a thug the next moment. The way he remained calm and controlled the situation had turned her on ever so slightly.

The group made it down to the VIP area without further incident. Everyone settled down on the couch nearest to them to watch the show. Sherrice and Darrell ended up on a huge couch with Terry and his date. Lashay ended up on another couch wedged between two crew members who were spitting some serious game at her. She loved the attention and it showed in the way she casually flirted with them.

Behind them the dome started to fill up. Everyone who was anyone in the 'Loo had come out in full force. Concerts of this caliber didn't come along this way often, so everyone was taking full advantage of flaunting their wealth and status. No one was flaunting harder than the GMC though.

Suddenly, the lights dimmed and the concert was underway. Sherrice snuggled closer to Darrell who was sipping on a pint of Hennessy that he passed back and forth with Terry. The Young Riders took the stage and the crowd went wild. They proceeded to rip through their underground hit entitled *"Let 'Em Have It."* Thirty GMC soldiers dressed in black GMC shirts stood behind them on stage tossing money into the air.

Darrell smiled and exchanged high fives with Terry. Their boys were ripping the stage and putting the GMC on the map at the same time. By the time The Young Riders finished, everyone in attendance was on their feet cheering. Their coming out party was complete and it was only a matter of time before the word spread and the major labels took notice.

Common took to the stage next. He did a few of his old classics before jumping into some of his newer material. The crowd got a nice surprise when Kanye and John Legend came from backstage and assisted him on *"They Say."* All three men were on top of their game and had the crowd in a frenzy.

When The Roots took the stage Sherrice excused herself to go to the bathroom. Darrell sent a security escort along with her. She didn't think she was in any danger, but after the episode with J-Ice earlier, anything was possible. The line to the ladies' room was long and wrapped around a corner. The security detail moved her to front of the line without hesitation. She could hear the women in the line wondering out loud who the fuck she was.

The men stayed outside while she went in to take care of business. She waited a few minutes before a stall came open. After she was done she went to the row of sinks along the wall to wash her hands. There were a few women already at the sinks, but she paid them no mind as she found an empty one.

"So you're his new bitch? I have to admit, you are pretty." The woman on her right suddenly stopped washing her hands and looked her up and down.

"Excuse me?" Sherrice looked over at the short brown-skinned sista dressed in tight blue jeans and a cute leather top. She didn't like her tone or the way she was looking at her.

"I'm Keke and Darrell is my babydaddy."

"Well thanks for the info, but that doesn't have shit to do with me." Sherrice dried her hands off and turned to leave only to find two other women blocking her path.

"Listen bitch, don't think you the shit cause you the current flavor of the month. Darrell always gets tired of his playthings and comes back to me. I just thought it was fair to warn you." Keke's girls came around to stand by her side and glare at Sherrice. "You may go now."

"Thanks for the advice, but if you call me a bitch again I don't care who you have with you. I'll beat your ass like you stole something from me. By the way, cute top." Sherrice turned on her heels and left the women standing in the restroom with their mouths wide open. She wasn't about to be intimidated by no silly hoes in a public bathroom. They had obviously mistaken her for a weak chick. She was Darrell's new girl now and she didn't plan on going nowhere.

Sherrice arrived back to her seat just as The Roots were playing through a hip version of their Grammy award winning song *"You Got Me."* Keyshia Cole had come from the back and was standing in on Erykah Badu's part. Sherrice sat down and started to sing along like nothing had happened at all. She kissed Darrell on the side of his face and put her hand in his.

John Legend was the next performer to take the stage. Sherrice loved the way his fingers glided over the keys on the piano. His sound reminded her of days gone by when her foster mother used to play old Sam Cooke and Donny Hathaway records in the afternoon. He sang a couple of his hits from both of his critically acclaimed albums.

Then it was time for Keyshia Cole to represent for the ladies. While she was going through her first few songs Sherrice looked over to the next couch to check on Lashay. Her friend appeared to be slightly tipsy and high. The thug sitting nearest to her had his tongue in

David Givens

her ear and his hand up under her short excuse for a dress. She was truly enjoying herself the best way she knew how.

Sherrice looked away, embarrassed for her friend. Couldn't she go out for once and just act like a real lady? She loved her friend, but wished she would have stayed at home. Her whorish ways would catch up to her one day and Sherrice hoped she wouldn't be around to see it. People tended to judge you based on the people you kept around you. She was going to have seriously reevaluate their friendship soon.

When Keyshia Cole wrapped up her performance by singing *"Love,"* everyone knew what time it was. It was well past midnight and the real show was about to begin. The man of the hour was about to perform. Suddenly the lights dimmed and fireworks started going off on the stage. The music for *"Jesus Walks"* filled the stadium; however no one knew where the Louis Vuitton Don was located.

Then an overhead spotlight came on and circled the crowd. Finally, it came to a halt in the VIP section. The light paused on the couch that held Darrell, Terry and their dates then it slid over slightly and Kanye West popped up from behind their couch with his mike in his hand. He quickly hugged them all before jumping onto the stage to join a choir and orchestra that had been

David Givens

hiding behind the curtain.

Sherrice was speechless with excitement. Kanye West hugged her! She stayed on her feet the whole time he performed. For two hours straight he took them on a roller coaster ride of his hits complete with outfit changes, smoke and a laser light show. The man really knew how to put on a show.

Darrell watched Sherrice's reactions out of the corner of his eye. It was nice to see that she was enjoying herself. Seeing her smile was well worth every penny he had shelled out on her. He could get used to seeing her smile on a regular basis.

David Givens

16

The concert after party was held at Darrell's soul food restaurant in its huge banquet room. Only the performers, their friends, GMC members and people cool with the GMC were allowed to enter. Sherrice was in utter shock to be standing elbow to elbow in a room full of stars. She had chatted earlier with Common about his role in the movie *"Smokin' Aces."* Now she was on the other side of the room talking to Keyshia Cole about her so called beef with Fantasia.

Darrell was in the back of the room talking with Kanye about old times. The Young Riders were nearby trying to soak up every word. Terry had snuck off to the meeting room in the back and was currently fucking his date on top of the table. Loco and Jay had ditched their dates for the night and were currently trying to go back to the hotel with two of Keyshia's back up dancers.

Lashay, on the other hand, was at home passed out on the bathroom floor. She lay there after vomiting into the toilet for the third time. Darrell had the limo driver take her home from the after party after she had embarrassed herself enough for the night. Apparently, she had tried to fight two members of Kanye's posse after they received blowjobs from her in the restaurant bathroom and laughed at her when she drunkenly asked them to pay her for her services.

The after party didn't wind down until around six in the morning. The only people left in the restaurant were Sherrice, Darrell and the clean up staff. Sherrice was seated at one of the tables going over the photos she had taken with Darrell's digital camera. She couldn't wait to upload them to her MySpace page. No one was going to believe the night she had.

Darrell sat with his arm around her shoulders smoking a blunt. The night had gone well from a business and personal standpoint. Kanye had told him to call his lawyers next week about getting The Young Riders signed to his label. If everything went according to plan this would be the first step in getting the GMC branched out into the music community. In another year or two he could probably start up his own label like Suge Knight or Irv Gotti.

David Givens

"I'm about to go over to the Ramada, did you want me to drop you off at home?" Darrell usually stayed in the penthouse suite on the weekends so he could get away from everything. The view from the tallest building in the city was breathtaking.

"Can I come with you? I don't feel like going home just yet." Sherrice knew Lashay was at home fucked up and she didn't want to deal with her.

"It's all good with me."

Darrell stood up and escorted Sherrice out the backdoor of the restaurant. His Benz was parked in the alley behind the building. He clicked off his alarm and opened the passenger side door for her. Once he got in they took off for the Ramada Inn a few streets over. Every now and then he would steal a glance over at her.

"Take a picture, it will last longer," Sherrice said as she stuck her tongue out at him.

"You got me." He smiled and stroked his goatee.

They pulled into the Ramada parking lot a minute later. Darrell got out, set his alarm and followed Sherrice through the automatic sliding front doors of the hotel. He couldn't help but to admire the way her ass looked in her dress. The bellboys and the men at the front desk couldn't help but to notice also. It made Darrell proud to know that his woman was causing all the men in the lobby to break their necks trying to get a look at her.

Once they were in the glass elevator Darrell swiped his key card in the slot provided and pressed the button for the top floor where the penthouse was located. Sherrice surprised him by sliding up close to him and wrapping her arms around his waist. He inhaled the sweet smell of her hair and hoped she couldn't feel his erection poking her in the stomach.

When they reached the top floor, Darrell's mind was full of conflict. He wanted to fuck Sherrice in the worst way, but on the other hand he would be disappointed if she let him. The time they were going to spend together in the hotel room was going to be a test. If Sherrice gave it up to him he would continue to fuck her for a while then get rid of her. He didn't want a serious relationship with a woman if she would give it up based on what he could give her. Now if she made him work for it then she was worth it. He hadn't met a woman yet who had made him work for it. So far Sherrice was holding her own.

Sherrice stared in amazement at the huge room they entered. It was at least twice the size of her apartment. There was a kitchen, living room, bedroom and a huge bathroom with a walk in shower and Jacuzzi. She walked around the room running her fingers over

David Givens

the expensive furniture. This was the type of living she could get used to.

She let out a small gasp when she saw the view from the window. The sun was halfway up over the city laid out below her. Orange and yellow streaks mingled with puffy white clouds in the morning sky. The scene was so peaceful.

Darrell came up behind her and wrapped her in his arms. She felt so safe in his embrace. Together they stood there in silence and watched the sun climb into the sky, as the city woke up. When they had seen enough they retreated into the bedroom to lie down. They were both equally exhausted from the previous day's events.

Sherrice slipped out of her dress and quickly got under the covers in the plush king-size bed. Darrell took his time taking off his shirt and slacks. He laid them on the nearest chair when he was done. While his back was turned, Sherrice admired his body. The muscles in his back rippled when he moved. His many tattoos gave his body a dangerous look.

When he turned around she noticed how his pecks looked like two huge slabs of black concrete. His stomach was flat and covered with a six pack that would make Tyson Beckford envious. Her eyes traveled down a little further to his boxers. The bulge in them let her know he was working with something very big.

Darrell climbed into the bed and lay on his back looking at the ceiling. Sherrice rolled over and lay on his chest listening to his heartbeat. He put his left hand behind his head while his right hand gently stroked her hair. Sherrice finally decided to break the silence.

"So Darrell, what is it that you do for a living?"

Darrell was slightly caught off guard by her question. "I'm a businessman."

"Don't bullshit me, Darrell. How many businessmen hang out with people like Terry? I also saw you stash that gun when we came in the room." Sherrice was looking him in the eye now.

"I'm sure the streets talk, so you probably know a little bit of what I do already. What do you want me to tell you?"

"I just want the truth. I'm really feeling you and I don't want there to be any secrets between us."

Darrell stared at Sherrice like she was crazy for a moment. She was asking him to trust her. In his line of work that was a hard thing to come by. Hell, he didn't even fully trust Terry. There were just some things that were best left unsaid.

"Listen, let me make this easy for you. I'm not asking you where the bodies are buried or if you slang coke. I just want to know if getting involved with you is

David Givens

safe?"

Darrell let out a sigh of relief. "Baby, there is no place safer on this Earth than by my side. As long as you got my back and stay loyal I'll treat you like the queen you deserve to be treated like." His left hand came down and stroked her face. "But...if you fuck me over, I'm not a very nice man."

"I can deal with that," she said as she kissed Darrell lightly on the lips and lay back down on his chest. Soon she was lightly snoring.

Darrell looked down at her and smiled. She had passed the test. He was really starting to like her. Now all he had to do was get this street business out the way. Soon he would be king of the streets and she would make the perfect queen.

17

Darrell's restaurant closed early on Monday after-noon. All the staff was gone, the blinds were drawn and the doors were locked. To someone passing by it looked like the place was empty. However, in the back there was a very important meeting going on that would turn the streets into a war zone.

The back meeting room was filled with all of Darrell's lieutenants within the GMC. Terry, Loco and Jay were present on one side of the table. Mo-Mo, Dwayne and Tre were on the other side. These men were Darrell's most loyal soldiers. They were the origi-nal members of the GMC. Now their crew had a mem-bership of just under two hundred men hustling in dif-ferent territories run by each of the lieutenants.

Terry, Loco and Jay each controlled the bulk of

Waterloo. Mo-Mo ran Evansdale, a small town right next to Waterloo that was mostly filled with middle class white people and a few blacks. Dwayne ran the upper west side of Waterloo. It was full of mostly rich people who influenced the community and loved to be discreet about their drug use. Tre ran Cedar Falls, Waterloo's sister city. It was a college city so drugs were a big part of the agenda there.

Darrell looked around the table at his men and nodded. They had come a long way and he was proud of them. Now it was time to move on to the next step. This would be their most dangerous plan yet, but he was confident they would pull it off without too many casualties.

"My niggas, we sit here on the verge of war. It's time for us to take over these streets and put some of these lame-ass niggas out of business. Now I know some of them won't go without a fight so we just gone have to lay them down."

"Which crews are we going up against?" asked Mo-Mo. He was a chubby light-skinned brother with braids.

"The City View Clique and the Crazy White Boys."

"Don't forget those bitch-ass L-Block Boys," Terry said from his seat.

"If they want it then them, too."

"Man, those Crazy White Boys is off the chain. They

got all kinds of weapons out at their farm," said Tre, a stocky brown-skinned brother from down south.

"Fuck them racist-ass crackers. I wouldn't get at them without bringing the heat." Darrell signaled for Loco to grab a crate in the corner. "Check this shit out."

Loco lugged the crate over to the table and cracked it open with a crowbar Darrell handed to him. A bunch of automatic and semi-automatic weapons spilled onto the floor. All the men got up and crowded around to get a better look. Darrell smiled and proceeded to grab a gun off the floor.

"I'm sure you are all familiar with the modified AK-47. I have over fifty of these at our warehouse. That over there is a HK53. It's a German assault rifle that comes with a forty round clip. I have thirty of those." Darrell paused for a moment to let his words sink in. "I know how you love shotguns, Terry. Check out that Mossberg 500, 20 gauge with the pistol grip. It's the same type the police use. I got around twenty of those."

"This is that shit I'm talking about," said Terry as he grabbed the shotgun and looked it over.

"Now check this shit out. You won't find too many of these out on the street." Darrell picked up a small rifle with a laser scope that looked like something out of a science fiction movie. "This is a Tavor-2. They are made in Israel. I got like ten of these. They work like a

David Givens

charm and the black rhino bullets that I got with them will go through any vest or armor plating."

"Don't you think this is overkill? I mean this shit is like for wars in third world countries or something," said Dwayne, a skinny cinnamon-toned brother with glasses and acne.

"Nigga, this is a war. If you want to be the best then you better have the best hardware," said Terry as he gave Loco a hi-five. "I'm ready to start putting holes in niggas right now."

Darrell nodded his head in agreement. He was happy that Carlos had come through for him. The weapons may have been more than enough, but he liked going into things over-prepared. He had also ordered a few more surprises that he would reveal at a later time.

"Now, I need for you to have your men put the word out on the street. Anyone in the L-Block Boys and The City View Clique that wants to make money can join on with us. If not then they can get out of town or be laid out in the morgue. As for those skin-headed punks in the Crazy White Boys, they can relocate or find a new hustle. They have been making too much money on our turf for too long. It's time we took over the Meth game, too."

Darrell hoped that the other crews would give up

without a fight and join them or leave. He knew that was just wishful thinking though. They would have to smoke a few motherfuckers before it was all said and done. Nothing ever came easy and it wasn't about to start now. That was just part of the game.

David Givens

18

"Who the fuck do those niggas think they are!" screamed Dwight Jansen. He punched the closest man to him in the mouth, knocking out a few of his teeth. "Everyone get the fuck out!"

All the men quickly found the nearest exits and left the angry man alone. When Dwight was angry, people tended to get shot. He sat alone in the office in the back of his three-storied house outside of Charles City that served as the headquarters of his operation. His left eye twitched and his breaths were coming in spurts.

Dwight was a large man with deeply tanned skin and huge muscles from years of steroid abuse. He kept his hair shaved close and his goatee long. Most people knew him as the racist leader of the Crazy White Boys. At the moment he was very pissed.

One of his men had come back from Waterloo beaten up with a message. Apparently, the GMC wanted them to move or to stop selling Meth in Waterloo. The nerve of those niggas! They got a little money and bought a few fancy cars and they thought they ran the world. This was ridiculous.

Dwight had never liked those black motherfuckers, but they all had an understanding. He didn't fuck with the crack and they didn't fuck with the Meth. Everyone made money and went home. Now those black bastards were getting greedy.

He looked out his window at the huge red farmhouse 500 yards away. It housed his giant Meth lab that was full of workers who produced the toxic drug night and day for him. He had two more houses and another farmhouse on his property that he used as living quarters for all his workers. They were currently supplying all of Northeast Iowa, Southern Minnesota and parts of Illinois. Business was booming and he was thinking of buying another farm.

He could probably live with not selling in Waterloo anymore. The amount of money he made there was just a drop in the bucket compared to the rest. However, he wasn't about to let some niggas tell him what to do. He was a fucking pure-blooded Aryan brother for Christ sakes!

David Givens

His fist slammed down on his desk so hard that the wood cracked. If the niggas wanted a war then he would give it to them. He hadn't been stockpiling guns and ammo on his farm for years just for show. The Sandman could go fuck himself for all he cared.

For now, he would have his men go into Waterloo in groups while they sold product. They would be supplied with guns and told to shoot any nigga that fucked with them. Once those monkeys saw that the Crazy White Boys couldn't be intimidated, they would probably back down. This would all blow over in a couple of days and he could move on and concentrate on bigger things.

* * * *

"Sammy and his boys just left and went over to the GMC this morning. That's about fifteen niggas that's left the crew this week. What do you want to do?" asked the young dark-skinned nigga with finger waves known as Hassan. His question was addressed to Lo-Key, the leader of the City View Clique.

Lo-Key took a moment to study the dart board across the room in his plush basement. He quickly fired off the three darts he held in his hand. They all clustered around the middle, but he didn't get a bull's-eye. "I suppose it was only a matter of time before those niggas started making power moves. Fuck them niggas that left and joined them. There's always a few rats in any organization."

Lo-Key talked tough, but on the inside he was scared to death and didn't really know how to react to the situation. He wasn't a thug nor had he really put in any real work in the streets. Lo-Key was just a young rich kid who surrounded himself with real niggas. Instead of being the lawyer or doctor his parents wanted him to be, he decided he wanted to be a criminal after watching countless reruns of *"New Jack City"* and *"King of NewYork."*

It seemed like his short run of being a wannabe gangsta was coming to an end. To make matters worse, word had gotten back to him that the Sandman knew he was shopping around for a new connect also. The only thing left for him to do would be to give up his spot and join the GMC or quit the game. However, he would look like a bitch in the eyes of those in his crew who stayed loyal.

His pride wouldn't allow him to go out like that. Lo-Key knew the next words out of his mouth would start him on a path that couldn't be changed once the going got tough. The slim fake gangsta quickly turned around and assumed his best hardcore pose. "These niggas want beef then they can get dealt with. Get our niggas together."

David Givens

Hassan shook his head as he left. He had been with Lo-Key since day one and knew that there wasn't a hardcore bone in his body. The smart decision would have been to join with the GMC. There was nothing to prove by going up against them. He also knew his boy was always worried about his image, but what good was an image when you were buried six feet deep?

* * * *

J-Ice sat in his living room playing John Madden Football on his PlayStation 3. The game looked great on his fifty inch flat screen television. A couple of his boys lounged around the room smoking weed and drinking Steel Reserve 211s. Rocky, J-Ice's right hand man was whipping J-Ice 24 to nothing.

Some of the guys in the room were visibly nervous. J-Ice hated to lose at anything. Last week some nigga on the corner beat him at dice and he shot the dude in the chest before taking all the money out the pot. Usually he was unbeatable at Madden, but his mind was somewhere else. Cats had been talking about the GMC taking over and he was not trying to hear that.

He would die before he saw the Sandman and Terry Law on top. Their recent antics were making it hard for small time niggas like himself to eat. He wasn't about to bow down and work for them niggas. Hell, they should be asking to work for him!

David Givens

A few of his boys had said they were going to join the GMC and he shot them on the spot. There would be no abandoning the ship over here. Once you were an L-Block Boy you were one for life. It was death before dishonor all the way.

J-Ice jumped up and turned off the television in the middle of the game. He wasn't about to lose at anything today. The whole room got quiet and all eyes were on him. Everyone tensed up and waited for what he was about to say.

"Fuck this pussy-ass shit. Them GMC motherfuckers ain't taking over shit. If they come on the L-Block then they getting wasted. Any nigga that want to be a bitch and run away or join them will be dealt with. Y'all niggas got any questions?"

"Terry Law is crazy as fuck. I'm not trying to run into that nigga," said a young soldier by the name of Tay. He was only fifteen and still wet behind the ears.

J-Ice walked over to his entertainment center and grabbed his gun off the shelf. He turned around and calmly walked over to Tay. The boy's eyes got big as he realized he had probably spoken his last words on this earth. J-Ice emptied his clip into the boy's body before he could even scream. Everyone around him ducked for cover behind pieces of furniture.

"I don't have time for scared niggas in my crew." J-

David Givens

Ice kicked Tay's lifeless body that was still smoking from the many bullets in it. "Now if any more of you want to say something stupid then raise your fucking hand." When no one spoke up J-Ice continued, "Now get this piece of shit's body out of here. And someone get me another beer."

19

Sherrice was having the time of her life. It had been two weeks since she had gone to the concert and everything was going well for her. The new job at the restaurant was fun and she was getting paid a nice chunk of change to do it. When Darrell wasn't busy he took her out on dates and out of town on shopping sprees. Her closets were filling up with designer clothing and shoes.

She was really feeling Darrell. He treated her like a princess when they were together and he never pressured her for sex. She never felt or looked better in her life. He kept her hair and nails done and made sure she kept money in her pocket. She didn't even have to spend the first check she got from work. It was deposited in her new back account untouched.

David Givens

Damn it felt good to have money in the bank for once!

The only thing that wasn't going too well was her relationship with Lashay. Ever since the concert her roommate had been acting funny toward her. She would say little slick shit under her breath all the time and steal Sherrice's clothing when she wasn't home. It got so bad that Sherrice had to put a lock on her door. Then there was the partying.

Lashay was just buck wild with it now. Sherrice would be awakened early in the mornings by loud music and a bunch of ruckus. When she would go to investigate she would find groups of people in her house engaged in sex acts, doing drugs or just plain sloppy drunk. Some of the people were rough looking and scared her. She could have sworn a few times some of the guys were from the L-Block Boys.

They would look at her with hungry eyes and she would quickly go into her room and lock the door. The situation was getting unbearable. She talked about it a few times with Lashay, but she would just laugh at her tell her that she paid half of the rent so she could do what she wanted to do. Sherrice wanted to call Darrell and tell him; however she didn't want him to think he had to save her all the time.

It was a Monday and Sherrice was just closing up the restaurant. They had made a lot of money for the day. When she was done adding up the receipts she handed the deposit bag to Bruno, one of the security people Darrell kept around. He would run it to the bank so she wouldn't worry about handling that type of money out at night.

When Sherrice stepped outside, the driver from the car service was just pulling up with the Lincoln Town Car. When she worked late Darrell would either pick her up or have the car service do it if he was busy. On the way home Sherrice left a sexy message on Darrell's answering machine. She hoped he would call her back as soon as he got in.

Her heart sank when the driver pulled up to her rundown building. Just coming home was starting to depress her now. Hopefully, she could change her living arrangement soon. She would talk to Darrell about it as soon as he called her back. For now she would have to deal with whatever surprise Lashay had in store for her.

On Mondays Lashay took the day off from the club, but she did do private parties at the crib to make some extra dough. Tonight was no different. Sherrice came in to the sound of loud music and the smell of weed. The sight before her almost made her drop her purse. Lashay was on her knees, buck naked, sucking two guys off at once.

David Givens

Sherrice recognized both guys right away. They were Rocky and Lucky, two of J-Ice's soldiers. She didn't like the way they stared at her whenever they came over. Both men looked up at her when she entered the room. She tried to hurry by as quick as possible, but Lashay turned around and just had to say something.

"Well if it isn't miss high and mighty." Lashay's words came out in a drunken slur. "You want to get in on this?"

"Yeah shortie, you got a phat ass. Why don't you come over here and let me show you what I'm working with?" Rocky grabbed his exposed dick and stroked it in Sherrice's direction.

Sherrice didn't even bother to say anything. She made a beeline for her room and locked the door as soon as she made it inside. That was the last straw. As soon as Darrell called her she was going to tell him to pick her up. There was no way she was living in this madhouse any longer.

"What's up with your home girl, she always act like she too good to get down?" asked Lucky.

"That bitch just think she the shit cause she fuck with the Sandman now."

"Word, that's the Sandman's chick?" Rocky exchanged a look with Lucky. This was too good to be

David Givens

true. "Why don't we make her join in on the action."

Sherrice had just laid her head down on her pillow when she heard the knob on her door jingling. She didn't think too much of it at first. Usually someone from one of Lashay's little parties always got confused and mistook her door for the bathroom door. They would give up after a few tries and stumble down the hallway to the right door. This time, however, her door was kicked in.

She sat up in time to see Rocky rushing into her room. The look in his eyes told her all she needed to know. She reached under her pillow for her mace, but he was too fast for her. His hand smacked her hard across the cheek causing her to fall back onto the bed. In a flash, he was on top of her with his hand over her mouth.

"So you're the Sandman's bitch? He must not care about you if he lets you live out in the slums. That's okay, old Rocky will take care of you."

Rocky started fondling her breasts with his free hand. He licked the side of her face making her want to gag. She could feel his hard dick pressed up against her belly. God, this couldn't be happening.

"I'm going to remove my hand. If you scream I'll beat the shit out of you. I just want to have a little fun then my man, Lucky, wants a turn. Hell, your girl

David Givens

Lashay said she might even want some." Rocky smiled wickedly as he removed his hand from her mouth. He then proceeded to unbutton her shirt.

Sherrice was scared out of her mind. She could hear her roommate out in the hallway laughing at her and egging Rocky on. This was all too much for her to handle. She never did anything wrong to anyone, so why was this happening?

Rocky had gotten her shirt open now. In one smooth motion he ripped her bra off exposing her beautiful breasts. He could hardly contain his excitement as he put one of her nipples into his mouth. Sherrice took this as her opening and reached under her pillow and grabbed her mace.

When Rocky looked back up at her he received a face full of mace. He screamed and clawed at his face in agony. Sherrice pushed him back and punched him with all her strength right in the mouth. He fell off the bed onto the floor and rolled around. Sherrice got up, grabbed her cell off the dresser and ran out her room. When she got into the hallway she saw Lucky and Lashay running toward her, blocking her path to the front door. She made it into the bathroom and locked the door just in time.

Lucky and Lashay started pounding and kicking on the door repeatedly. She didn't know how long she would be able to keep them out. Sherrice put her entire weight on the door as she dialed Darrell's number. She hoped he would answer in time or she was probably a goner. There was no way Rocky was going to let her slide for macing him.

Darrell had just left the club. He had been out all night partying with Loco and Jay. For some reason no one could get in touch with Terry. He was probably busy with a new ho or out in the streets making sure everything was running smoothly. Terry was well known for his disappearing acts.

Darrell was cruising down the street on the lower east side in his Benz listening to a DJ Clue mixtape. His vibrating phone made him lower the volume. He saw that it was Sherrice's number and put it on speaker phone. She probably just wanted to wish him a good night.

"What's up baby?"

"Darrell, help me. They're trying to rape me!" Sherrice's terrified voice filled the cabin of the car. Darrell could hear the banging and yelling in the background.

"Who is, baby?"

"Some niggas from the L-Block. Lashay is helping them. You got to get here. Oh shit..." The line went

David Givens

dead as Darrell went into a rage.

Since he was already on the east side he was close to her. He whipped his car around in an illegal U-turn and headed for her apartment. Everything became a blur as he weaved in and out of traffic. He would die if anything happened to her.

Darrell pulled up to the apartment and screeched to a halt three minutes later. He made sure he grabbed his nine and his silencer out of his secret stash box. In a few seconds he was already flying up the stairs. He didn't even pause when he came upon her door. He just hoped the deadbolt wasn't set when he lowered his shoulder and hit it dead on.

Sherrice had tried to hold the bathroom door as long as she could, but it finally burst open. Lucky burst in and smacked her cell out of her hand. He then proceeded to beat her to the floor with a series of blows. She blocked most of them with her arms, but a few got through. Then he grabbed her by her hair and dragged her out into the hallway.

Rocky had recovered a little by this time and he came over and started stomping her with his Timberlands all in her back. The pain was unbearable. She was barely conscious, but she could hear Lashay in the background laughing at her and calling her a

David Givens

stuck up bitch. When both men started grabbing at her clothes she knew they were probably going to rape her and then kill her.

Suddenly, the front door exploded off its hinges. Everyone stopped what they were doing and looked. The Sandman came flying through the door like a raging bull. He leaped through the air and tackled Lucky and Rocky to the floor at the same time. Lashay jumped on his back and he knocked her across the room like she was a rag doll. She hit the wall and lay on the floor in a daze.

He then grabbed Lucky and pulled him up to his feet. Lucky threw a couple of weak punches at Darrell, but he brushed them off like they were nothing. Darrell started working the smaller man over with the skill of a seasoned boxer. Every punch sounded like a sledgehammer hitting a brick wall. Soon Lucky was a bloody mess that was only being held up by Darrell's fists. Darrell let him fall down to the floor in a heap. He then turned his attention toward Rocky.

Rocky was on the floor still out of it from the mace and being tackled. He looked up in time to see a size thirteen boot coming down on his face. Darrell stomped him in his face until it caved in and made squishy sounds. Then Darrell pulled out his nine and walked back over to Lucky. He stood over him silent-

David Givens

ly while he screwed on the silencer.

"Come on man, you made your point. I don't want to die," said Lucky as he cried and tried to back away.

"What's your name," asked Darrell.

"They call me Lucky."

"Well I guess today your luck just ran out." Darrell emptied two hot ones right into Lucky's head. He watched his body twitch for a moment before it lay still.

Next, Darrell walked back over to Rocky. He was barely breathing and would probably die without medical attention. There would be no mercy for him tonight though. Darrell put two in his brain also. The Sandman had put two more niggas to sleep.

Darrell turned and rushed to Sherrice's side. She had sat up by now and was trying to look around. Her back hurt and she had a few light bruises on her face. Darrell put his gun away and picked her up in his strong arms. He carried her down to his Benz and laid her down in the back seat.

When he was sure that she was alright he closed the door and set his alarm. He walked back up to the apartment and surveyed the damage. The place was a bloody mess. Lashay lay in the corner whimpering with wide, frightened eyes. He shook his head at the trifling bitch and whipped out his cell phone. Terry answered after the fourth ring.

"What's up nigga, is everything okay?"

"Some shit done come up. I have a situation. I need you and a couple of the guys to come through at Sherrice's spot for a clean up."

"Word, do I have to bring extra heat?"

"Naw, ain't shit moving over this way anymore. Just bring some cleaning supplies and a junk car over."

"Alright, see you in ten." Terry put his phone back on the nightstand and tapped the woman that was giving him head on the shoulder. "Yo, I have to go and take care of some business. I'll probably be gone for the rest of the night so let yourself out."

Terry jumped out of bed and rushed to put his clothes on. He made a few phone calls while he searched for his shoes. Then he came back to the bed and kissed the woman on the forehead. She grabbed his shirt and pulled him lower so she could French kiss him.

"Damn girl, don't be doing me like that when I have to leave. I can't be going out with my dick all rock hard," laughed Terry as he playfully pushed her back on the bed and headed for the door.

"Call me later," said Keke as she lay in the bed and watched him leave.

David Givens

Terry went outside and jumped into his midnight blue Dodge Charger. He knew it was wrong to be fucking Darrell's babymomma, but her head game was just too good to pass up. Besides, what Darrell didn't know wouldn't hurt him. He started the car up and sped off into the night on his way to help out his boy.

20

Darrell woke up the next day feeling a little on edge. He never enjoyed killing people, but sometimes it was just a part of the job. Things tended to get out of hand in the streets sometimes. It was a cold world he operated in and sometimes you had to be even colder to deal with it all.

He rolled out of his huge bed and walked down the hallway toward the spare room he put Sherrice in last night. He peeked in the door and saw her sleeping peacefully. She looked like an angel. He couldn't believe that he had almost lost her last night.

The guilt hit him like a ton of bricks. He should have been moved her out the hood, but he didn't want to pressure her. Now his slow reactions had caused her to get hurt. From now on he was taking over this rela-

David Givens

tionship and letting her know how he felt. He had reached a point where he could finally admit to himself that he was falling in love with this woman. Now he had to let her know.

At least he knew she was going to be okay. Late last night he had one of his doctor friends come over and check her out. She would have a few slight bruises for awhile, but she would make a speedy recovery. Now he just had to wait and see how she reacted. There was no telling what type of trauma her mind suffered through the whole ordeal.

"Are you going to stare at me all morning or are you going to come in and talk to me?" Sherrice sat up in the bed and smiled at him.

Darrell entered the room and sat down on the bed beside her. She looked so sexy wearing one of his T-shirts. He leaned over and kissed her softly on the lips. She hugged him tightly around the neck and looked into his eyes.

"Thank you for saving me last night. It seems like you are always there when I need you."

"It should have never had to be that way. It's all my fault. I should have been moved you up here."

"Don't say that. Everything happens for a reason. Now, did I just hear you say that you want me to move in?"

David Givens

"Yeah, it's long overdue. You're my woman now and I can't have you out in the hood like some chicken head. That's just not right. From now on think of my home as your home."

"Thank you so much. I don't know what to say."

"You just get some rest. I have you on paid leave from work for two weeks. You can relax around the house and do you. If you need to go somewhere hit me on my cell or call the car service. Things might get a little dangerous over the next few days."

"You think J-Ice will try something?"

"I know he will."

"You be careful then. I don't want anything to happen to you either."

"I'm always careful. Now get some rest and I'll check in on you later. If you need anything to eat use the phone on the nightstand. Dial 1 and the chef will pick up. He can fix you anything you want." Darrell kissed Sherrice again and exited the room.

He went over to his study and sat down in his expensive leather chair. His actions from last night replayed over in his mind. Terry and a few of the crew members had shown up a few minutes after he called. They went to work quickly on cleaning the apartment and getting rid of all the evidence.

The bodies were dismembered in the bathtub and

David Givens

the pieces were wrapped up in a blanket and carried out to a stolen car. Darrell thought about busting a cap in Lashay too, but she wasn't worth it. The trifling ho knew what time it was. She wouldn't tell a soul anything or she would wind up on a milk carton.

Darrell and his crew left after his locksmith friend showed up to fix the door. They took the stolen car over by the Cedar River and drove it off a bridge. The bricks in the trunk made it sink quickly. Everyone drove off in a separate direction after that. It was an old drill that his crew knew all too well.

Now Darrell had to sit back and see how the situation played itself out. J-Ice was sure to want revenge. There was no telling what the little punk would do. Darrell wasn't about to walk around scared though. He feared no man and was always ready for whatever. It looked like the little war he was planning was about to pop off a little early. Let the games begin.

21

Detective Thomas sat inside the Black's Cafe on Sycamore Street eating an egg salad sandwich on rye while sipping on a cup of strong, black coffee. He had been up early once again going over a crime scene. Bodies were starting to pop up in the oddest places. The whole thing was starting to give him a migraine.

The funny thing about the latest discovery was that he had received an anonymous phone call telling him where to find the bodies. However, the phone call was on his unlisted home phone. The voice was disguised like the person was using a distortion device. He could-n't tell if it was a man or a woman.

He decided to check out the tip anyway. Of course when he sent divers into the river early that morning they found a car that had been reported stolen two

David Givens

days ago. When the crane pulled the car out they found a grisly surprise waiting for them inside the trunk. Two dismembered bodies were wrapped in a blanket. The hands were gone and the faces were a mess so there would be no identifying them.

The caller had stated that the GMC was involved with the murder, but with no evidence or identities the case was a dead end. Malik was frustrated to say the least. The caller had to know that he wouldn't be able to do anything with the bodies. Then an idea came to mind.

The caller hadn't called to help with the case. This was something bigger. The media would get a hold of the discovery and whoever did the crime would know that the bodies were found. This would probably cause them to go looking for the snitch in their crew.

So apparently there was another player in the game. Malik smirked at the idea. He wondered who the GMC pissed off and how could he use it to his advantage. Any enemy of his enemy was his friend. Things were starting to look better already.

Malik got up and paid for his food. It was time to go to the station and get started on his mountain of paperwork. He left a nice tip for the cute waitress and he was out the door. The slight breeze outside felt good on his skin as he walked over to his car. He had a good feel-

David Givens

ing that the phone call he received was the first of many. Yes, it was a good day indeed.

J-Ice pulled his Tahoe up to a beautiful mansion surrounded by a giant iron fence on the outskirts of town. He hated driving all the way out to the lovely estate. It reminded him of all the luxuries he grew up without. After two burly security guards checked his identification and underneath his truck, the gate was opened and he was allowed to drive up the sprawling driveway toward the mansion.

He parked his vehicle in between a black Bentley Flying Spur and a gray Rolls-Royce Phantom. Both cars combined were worth more than he had made hustling in his entire life. The huge main door opened before he made it halfway up the stairs. Two more huge security guards ushered him into a small foyer were they patted him down and removed his gun.

Then he was led to a huge study to wait for the man of the house. He was left alone, but he knew the place was bugged and full of surveillance cameras. Every wall in the study was covered with built in bookshelves. There had to be at least a couple thousand books crammed on them. The room smelt of furniture polish and cigar smoke.

Soon the door at the other end of the room opened

David Givens

and two personal bodyguards came in. They looked like two brick walls in suits pretending to be people. They were followed by a tall dark skinned man with sad eyes. He wore a gray cashmere turtleneck with charcoal slacks. The Gucci loafers on his feet and the planet-sized rock on his finger were the only indicators of his wealth.

The man sat down behind a huge mahogany desk. His bodyguards stood on either side of him with grim looking faces. He reached for a box on his desk and removed a Cuban cigar. One of his bodyguards lit it for him and he took a long drag. When he exhaled he finally looked in J-Ice's direction.

"So my wayward nephew decides to pay me a visit. I can tell this isn't a social call since you only come by when you want something. This wouldn't have anything to do with the Sandman, now would it?" asked the man known to everyone as the Minister.

"How did you know?" J-Ice was always amazed at his uncle's ability to seemingly know everything that went on in the streets.

"You must have forgotten whom you were talking to, boy. There is nothing that goes on in this city that I don't know about."

"Then you know that motherfucker killed Rocky and Lucky. I can't let that shit ride. Those were my dogs."

David Givens

"Watch your damn mouth when you are in my home, boy. Act like you have some house training. I'm sorry to hear about your friends, but what do you want me to do?" The Minister flicked out his ashes into a gold plated ashtray nearby.

"I want you to give me the okay to take that nigga off the face of this Earth."

The Minister was quiet for a moment. The only sound in the room was the flicking of ashes and the ticking of an antique clock in the corner. J-Ice screwed up his face and wondered why his uncle was taking so long with his response. It wasn't that difficult of a decision in his opinion. The nigga had killed his boys and now he had to kill him. The only reason he was asking for his uncle's blessing was because he knew his uncle wasn't down with too much havoc in his streets.

The Minister finally handed his cigar to one of his bodyguards who promptly put it out and returned the unused part back into its box. "I can't give you my blessing on that one, nephew."

"What the fuck do you mean!" J-Ice screamed as he shot to his feet with his fists balled up. "This is some bullshit." He sat back down when the biggest bodyguard displayed the automatic pistol tucked in his waistband.

"Boy, sit down and shut your damn mouth. This is a

          David Givens

complicated situation that is a whole lot bigger than your petty beef. You do know that your boys were trying to rape the man's woman. He was justified in taking their asses out."

"Fuck that shit. His girl is a ho. She probably set them up. An eye for eye is the only way. I can't look weak out in these streets."

"I told you to watch your tongue! Keep disrespecting my house and you will be dealt with accordingly. There are things in motion already that you don't understand. There is a street war on the horizon. Its outcome interests me to a great degree."

"You talking about the GMC trying to take over?"

"Exactly, if the Sandman is successful then I won't have so many different knuckleheads to keep in check. Besides he understands business unlike some of you crazy fools out here bringing down the property value with your loud cars and childish antics. He'll be a lot easier to control in the long run. You understand this is only business?"

"So you saying that you would choose some bitch-ass nigga over your own nephew just because he runs a few businesses and dresses nice? I can't believe this shit. Mother said you were foul, but this is some bullshit for real."

"Don't you ever mention your mother around me.

She chose the life she lived. You're lucky I even deal with your disrespectful ass. If my blood wasn't in your veins I wouldn't have anything to do with you."

"You act like I need you—the high and mighty Minister. Everything I've built has been by myself and I don't need your blessing to take that nigga out. Fuck you and your status. That nigga is dead. That's my word." J-Ice jumped up and turned to leave.

The Minister's bodyguards moved to stop him, but the Minister put his hand up. He was tired of having to deal with his nephew. He was tired of being reminded of his long dead sister. It was time to let the boy become a man. Another hand gesture told the body-guards to leave the room.

The Minister sat alone in his study and watched J-Ice speed down his driveway through his window. A barely audible sigh escaped his lips. The boy was stubborn just like his mother once was. The Minister's younger sister had been shunned by the family years ago. She shacked up with a young hustler, breaking their father's heart. He had wanted her to be a lawyer or be deeply involved in the church. Her decision proved to be a fatal one when she was killed in a drive-by that was meant for her boyfriend.

No one even knew she had a baby up until a few years ago. The Minister was shocked to learn he had a

David Givens

nephew growing up right under his nose. He tried to reach out to him, but the boy had already been turned by the ways of the street. The only thing he could do was to make sure people knew that the boy was under his protection. Now he couldn't protect him any longer. If J-Ice went up against the Sandman and failed then it would mostly likely mean death.

Life had a funny way of repeating itself. The Minister got up and walked over to one of his many bookshelves. He found the book he was looking for and removed it. The tiny book with the tattered cover was his younger sister's old diary. He had found it years ago when he was cleaning out his father's house after moving him into a retirement facility. One single tear fell from the Minister's eye onto the cover. He knew in his heart that he had failed his sister once again.

22

A few weeks had passed and Sherrice was back to her old self. She was working again and enjoying life. Currently, she was cruising down the street listening to *"The Evolution of Robin Thicke"* in her brand new BMW 750Li. The car was a beautiful pearl white color with a peanut butter leather interior. A set of chromed out 22-inch rims set it off.

A couple days ago Darrell had surprised her with the car. She had been sleeping in the house when he woke her up and told her to come outside. When she saw the beautiful car with a giant red ribbon around it she almost fainted. Tears ran down her face as she took the keys from him and checked the whole car over.

Later on that day she surprised him in his study. They had been together for a few months and Darrell had taken very good care of her. She lived in a house that looked like something on "*MTV Cribs*," had a huge walk-in closet full of designer clothing and shoes, had money in the bank and now he had given her a very expensive car. Not once had he ever tried to come at her wrong. He had let her into his world and now she decided it was time to give herself to him completely.

She found him in his study reading an old novel by Richard Wright. It always amazed her to see the many different sides of him. He sensed her presence and looked up. She only wore a black bra and a matching thong. The surprise and hunger was evident on his face.

She came to him and he quickly set down his book. Her soft kisses had him breathing hard in no time. He pushed her down onto a couch in the corner and stood over her. She watched him undress slowly. His body was so rough and powerful looking. The overhead lighting made his tattoos seem to jump off his skin. He was her chocolate Adonis with the fiery eyes.

She ran her fingers across his hard six-pack and pulled down his boxers. His dick was huge even at rest. She took him into her mouth and heard him gasp in surprise as she swallowed up his manhood down to the balls. His dick swelled and expanded, but she was still able to handle all nine inches. When he was super rock hard she stopped.

He stared down at her with so much passion it almost scared her. When he got down on his knees, removed her thong and spread her legs she knew what time it was. He licked and sucked her clit so good she thought she had died and gone to heaven. She climaxed at least three times before he came up for air.

Then he was on top of her. He rubbed his huge dick head around her clit, teasing her. She finally had enough and reached down to shove it in. There were a brief few seconds of pain as she adjusted to his size. A moan escaped her lips as he filled her up. He stroked her slowly with her legs on his shoulders.

After a while they switched positions and she ended up on top riding him fast and furious. He flung her bra to the floor and sucked on her breasts as she bounced up and down on his dick. His giant hands palmed her ass as they grinded together. She was loving the way he made her feel.

Eventually she found herself bent over the couch with Darrell ramming her hard from behind. He occasionally slapped her ass while he thrust away like a madman. She felt him tense up as she was going for her sixth orgasm. He exploded inside her as she came. They both collapsed to the floor in a big heap. She liked watching the way his chiseled chest rose and fell as he

David Givens

tried to catch his breath. Afterwards they showered together and had another steamy session of lovemaking underneath the cascade of water. He told her he loved for the first time while he was toweling her off.

The sweet memory made Sherrice blush as she maneuvered her car through traffic. She stopped at a small health food store on Falls Avenue and jumped out the car looking like a runway model. Her Versace outfit and Manolo pumps complemented the Louis Vuitton purse hanging on her arm. A couple men walking down the street stopped and stared. She was killing 'em and she knew it.

She entered the store and proceeded all the way to the back. That's where they kept the sunflower seed cookies. She had tasted some once at a job fair a few years back and had been hooked ever since. They were her secret pleasure. She had just grabbed two bags off the shelf when something grabbed her leg.

"Hi Auntie Sherrice, is Daddy with you?" Darrell Jr. was hugging her leg looking up at her with the sweetest smile she had ever seen.

She had grown close to the child in the past few weeks. Darrell had brought him over a few times and they had done some family outings together. They had bonded over time spent in the park, at movies and at Chuck E. Cheese. His mother didn't like it one bit and she called to tell Darrell about every chance she got. Sherrice wondered where the wannabe diva was lurking.

"Well don't you look nice," said Keke as she came around the corner and looked Sherrice up and down. "Darrell, get your hands off that lady and come over here. I don't want you catching anything."

Sherrice rolled her eyes. "That's real mature. Anyway, I'll see you this weekend, Darrell. You be a good boy."

"Don't be talking to my son like you know him. You'll be out of his life just as soon as his father gets tired of your ho ass." Keke followed Sherrice to the register pulling her son behind her.

"You mean like when he got tired of you? I believe you were the one caught cheating, right?" Sherrice smirked as she paid for her items and exited the store.

Keke stormed outside after her filled with anger. She had been following Sherrice around all day just looking for a chance to provoke her and now she was the one getting mad. Jealousy had consumed her. As far as she was concerned the bitch in front of her was sleeping with her man, wearing her clothes, driving her car and now trying to win over her son. The shit had to end.

Sherrice had just opened the door to her car when

David Givens

she felt a tap on her shoulder. She turned to see a hand coming at her face. The slap didn't hurt, it just surprised her. This bitch was actually attacking her in broad daylight with her son beside her. This was some Jerry Springer shit for real.

"Now what, bitch. You talking all that tough talk, but you ain't shit." Keke was all in her face now. Her son stood a foot away with tears in his eyes.

"Keke, take your son and go home. I am not trying to fight you out here on some stupid shit. I'm with Darrell now, so you just have to deal with it. Get a life." Sherrice wanted to fuck Keke up, but she was concerned about Darrell Jr. She didn't want to beat his mother up in front of him.

"You don't tell me what to do. I knew you were just a scary ho anyway. Stupid orphan bitch." Keke cocked her head to the side and put her hand on her hip daring Sherrice to do something.

Sherrice put her bag in the car and tried to calm her nerves. It was no use though. The bitch had gone too far. Her upbringing was always a sensitive subject. Darrell Jr. was just going to have to be traumatized. She turned around and punched Keke dead in her eye.

Keke staggered back in shock. Before she could recover she was hit two more times in the head. The pavement came up to meet her as she fell hard on her

David Givens

side. Sherrice was on top of her punching and clawing away like a wild animal. Darrell Jr. was somewhere in the distance crying. *Maybe it wasn't such a good idea to fuck with her,* thought Keke as blows rained down upon her head.

Suddenly, Loco and Jay appeared. Darrell had them secretly shadowing Sherrice lately to make sure nothing happened to her. They could have stopped the fight from happening, but they weren't Keke's biggest fans. Besides, it got boring following a chick around all day. This was the most exciting thing they had witnessed all week. They pulled Sherrice off Keke and made her get in her car.

"Didn't I tell you to watch who you called bitch? Now look at you—all fucked up." Sherrice spit out the window of her car onto Keke's face. Then she put her Chole shades on and sped out of the parking lot.

Jay helped Keke to her feet. Once she got up she snatched her hand away from him and staggered toward her son. "I don't need your fucking help. That bitch is lucky I slipped. Shit, she lucky you two showed up when you did. I was just about to get her off me and beat her down."

Loco and Jay looked at each other and then back at Keke. She stood beside her crying son with a black eye and a busted lip. Her weave was hanging halfway off

David Givens

her head and her shirt was ripped. They couldn't help but to laugh at her.

"Yo, you need to take your son home and get fixed up. How you gone be fighting out here with your son anyway?" asked Loco in between his laughter.

"I do what I feel. I'm not done with that bitch yet."

"I wonder how the Sandman will feel about you harassing his shortie?" said Jay.

"Fuck that nigga and his bitch. I ain't scared of him."

"Then you won't mind telling him that cause he's on my cell right now." Loco held his cell phone out toward Keke.

Her whole face changed and her lip started trembling. If Darrell had heard a word of what she just said then the beat down she just received would be nothing compared with what he would do to her. She picked up her son and beat a hasty retreat back to her beat up Chevy Malibu. Both men fell out into another fit of laughter as she sped off. Loco's phone hadn't even been on.

23

Darrell closed his cell phone and stormed out of one of the gas stations he owned. Loco had just informed him of the fight between Keke and Sherrice. He knew Keke was jealous, but he didn't know she would take it that far. And to be fighting in front of his son, what the fuck was she thinking?

He called Keke's cell and immediately got sent to the voicemail. She probably cut her phone off cause she knew he would call. He left her a message telling her to stay away from Sherrice and to stop putting his son in the middle of crazy shit or he would take him from her. His threat was real. He had been thinking of getting full custody lately anyway. Keke was too much of a party girl to be a good mother. Besides, he enjoyed how it made him feel to have Sherrice and his son

David Givens

together in the same house.

Darrell leaned up against the side of his Infiniti truck and took a swig of the Gatorade he swiped from the gas station. The discovery of Rocky and Lucky's bodies a few weeks ago had him thinking. Only his crew knew where the bodies were dumped. However, someone could have seen them also. He just didn't like the idea of someone being able to tie him to a crime scene. He'd have to keep a closer eye on some of his crew members. There was always someone out to dethrone the king.

He took his cell out again and dialed Sherrice's number. She picked up on the first ring.

"Why do you have Jay and Loco following me around?"

"Hello to you too." Darrell smiled to himself. He loved her fire.

"I suppose you heard about my little fight with your babymomma?"

"More like you beat her ass."

"She had it coming. The bitch attacked me with your son by her side."

"I know, I'll handle it. She'll never bother you again."

"You better make sure your son is okay. It's not cool to see your mother catch a beat down. He may not like me for awhile."

"I'll make him understand. I just wanted to make sure you're okay."

"I'm fine. Now are you going to tell me why your boys are following me around? I'm too grown for babysitters."

"The situation with J-Ice hasn't been taking care of yet. I can take care of myself, but I can't leave you alone out in the open."

"You think it's that serious? I mean his boys were trying to rape me or worse."

"That doesn't matter out here in these streets, baby. I killed his boys and he has to retaliate. He wouldn't be much of a man if he didn't."

"Well fix this shit soon. I don't want to be looking over my shoulder or worrying about you everyday. I love you and I'll see you at home later."

"I love you too."

Darrell put his cell away and finished his Gatorade. The sun was shining and a nice breeze had just begun. He just turned to toss his empty bottle into a nearby trash bin when he caught a blur of movement out the corner of his eye. The sound of automatic gunfire turned the peaceful day into chaos.

Darrell instinctively dropped to the ground and rolled over reaching for the .22 in his ankle holster.

David Givens

Bullets sprayed the outside of his truck where he was standing a few seconds before. He heard the screeching of tires on the pavement. When he rose back to his feet with his gun in hand he saw a green Tahoe speeding off into the distance.

People came running out of the gas station and the surrounding neighborhood to see what had happened. Darrell put his gun away and looked himself over. His blue Enyce shirt was ruined and his knee was banged up, but he was okay. His truck was okay too. The bulletproof paneling and glass were a good investment.

He couldn't believe that he had been caught slipping in broad daylight. His .22 wouldn't have been much of a match against an automatic weapon unless the person got careless and too close. Lucky for him his would-be killer was too stupid to get out and finish the job they started. There was only one person he knew with a green Tahoe like the one that was driven by the person who tried to gun him down. J-Ice had just bought himself a one way ticket to hell.

Detective Thomas pulled up to the gas station on Newell Street and fired up a Newport fresh out of his new pack. He exited the car and walked over to check out the crime scene. As usual, there were too many people floating around. It seemed like the whole neigh-

David Givens

borhood had emptied out and crowded around the gas station. *Damn nosey-ass people.*

A few cops worked the crowd looking for witnesses. Malik knew they would find none. A couple lab guys ran around taking pictures and picking up spent ammo casings and bullets. He wasn't interested in them either. The man Detective Thomas was looking for was standing off to the side having a heated discussion on his cell phone.

Darrell looked up as Detective Thomas approached. He cut his phone conversation short and frowned. Both men hated each other.

"What the fuck are you doing here? This isn't a homicide."

"I work the gang unit also. You know how much I like to multi-task."

"Well I don't know shit, so you're wasting your time."

"Oh I didn't come to ask any questions. I'm pretty sure this little misunderstanding has something to do with J-Ice. Word on the street is you two have beef."

"I don't do beef. I'm a businessman, Detective. You remember what happened last time you started throwing around accusations. I don't think the police force can handle another lawsuit at the moment."

"Play your little game all you want to, motherfucker.

David Givens

I'm on to you. It's only a matter of time before you or your pal Terry slips up." The detective stepped closer to Darrell and looked him straight in the eye. "Enjoy the ride for now. I'll be waiting for you when it's over." Malik blew smoke in Darrell's face and walked off.

It took everything in Darrell not to fuck the crooked-ass cop up. He didn't need this shit right now. There was too much at stake to let some nappy-headed jealous-ass cop get to him. He walked back to his truck and got in. The police were done photographing it.

Before he could pull off, Detective Thomas pulled up next to him in his unmarked sedan.

"By the way, nice truck," the detective smirked as he drove off slowly.

Darrell gave him the finger.

24

J-Ice was living on borrowed time and he knew it. It had been two days since his failed attempt on the life of the Sandman. Since then, more than half of his crew had either left town or joined ranks with the GMC. The other half started showing up dead across the city. There were numerous drive-bys and home invasions. The streets were raining with blood and he didn't have a raincoat.

They took everything from him. His drugs spots were raided and his apartment set on fire. Even his babymommas didn't want anything to do with him. He couldn't leave the city since they had people watching the airport, bus terminal and the highways. It was like some bad dream.

He called the Minister a couple of times, but the

David Givens

person on the other end kept saying he wasn't in. After the fifth call the number was disconnected. Now he was alone and scared running through a cornfield in the middle of the night. He only moved at night so he could stay in the shadows. There was no way they were watching the fields. If he could get far enough out in the country he could get around the people they had watching the highways and catch a ride.

His boy from Milwaukee named Terence was supposed to be meeting him on a dirt road out in the middle of nowhere. It was a road not listed on any map. Hopefully, it was safe. He was paying Terence two grand to get him up out of hell.

He paused as he got to the edge of the field. His gun was clutched firmly in his hand. Sweat covered his face and made his dirt covered clothing stick to him. If he lived through this he was seriously going to join a gym and lose some weight.

A set of headlights appeared in the distance traveling toward him. He took a flashlight out of his pocket and flashed it on and off twice. The headlights did the same. So far so good. It looked like he was going to make it. When he got to Milwaukee he was going to lay low for a while and stay with some family. Hopefully, he would be able to get a new crew together and come back for revenge. The Sandman hadn't heard the last of

David Givens

him.

The headlights came closer and J-Ice could make out the outline of a minivan. It stopped a few feet away from him and the headlights switched off. A lone figure stepped out of the vehicle and approached him. I appeared to be Terence, but he couldn't make out the face.

"Terence, is that you?"

"Who else would it be? Get your ass out of the corn and let's get the fuck out of here. Got me out here on this spooky-ass road in the middle of the night."

J-Ice recognized his boy's voice and relaxed. He tucked his gun in his waistband and stepped out onto the road. Everything was going to be all right. At least that's what went through J-Ice's mind as he hugged his friend.

"I'm sorry," Terence whispered as he embraced his friend.

The sliding doors on the minivan slid open and four men dressed in black with ski masks on jumped out. J-Ice pushed his friend out the way and went for his gun only to find that it was gone. His boy had set him up and snatched his gun while they hugged. He was a sitting duck.

Panic filled J-Ice's heart as he ran for his life. He didn't get far before one of the men tackled him to the

David Givens

ground. Then they were on him punching and kicking away. They beat him senseless for close to ten minutes. Finally they stopped and one of the men bent down over him and removed his ski mask so J-Ice could see his face.

"So you thought you were going to get away, fat boy?" Terry looked down on him and smiled wickedly. "No one ever gets away from us."

Terry stood up and laughed at him. His laughter sent chills down J-Ice's spine. Then one of the other men handed Terry an aluminum baseball bat. He raised it high in the air and brought it down on the side of J-Ice's head. Everything went black after that.

J-Ice was awakened by a bucket of freezing water thrown in his face. He coughed and sputtered. His body felt like he had been hit by a train. The side of his head felt even worse. He opened one of his swollen eyes and tried to look around.

As his senses came back to him he noticed that he was naked. His arms were painfully handcuffed behind his back and his feet were bound with heavy rope. He wasn't dead, but that didn't mean it was a good thing. A lone figure was sitting in a chair before him. As his vision came into focus he realized that the Sandman was sitting in front of him wearing a suit and drinking coffee.

David Givens

"You know, you're even fatter than I realized. A fat, stupid motherfucker. Did you really think you could try and kill me and get away with it?"

"Man, either kill me or let me go." J-Ice was having trouble talking. His jaw was swollen to twice its normal size.

"Tough talk from a pussy-ass nigga. I like that though. It shows you have heart. Not a lot of brains, but some heart."

Darrell got up from his chair and put down his coffee. He had two men stand J-Ice up as he loosened his tie and walked up to him. Another man helped him out of his suit coat and handed him a set of brass knuckles. After cracking his neck he slipped the brass knuckles on and went to work on J-Ice's flabby body. Each powerful blow lifted the fat thug off the ground.

When Darrell got tired he put the brass knuckles away and grabbed a towel from one of his men. J-Ice lay on the floor whimpering like a baby and spitting up blood. A few of his ribs were broken and he had pissed himself. He was in very bad shape.

"Today is your lucky day, motherfucker. I'm feeling pretty good so I'm going to let you go. No one can say that I don't have a kind heart," said Darrell as he toweled the sweat from his brow.

He gestured toward the two men who were holding

David Givens

J-Ice. They uncuffed him and cut the rope from his legs. When he tried to stand, he fell back down to the floor. His body was just too spent. The two men roughly picked him up and half dragged, half carried him toward what he thought was the exit. When they stopped, J-Ice looked around and realized he was standing on a ledge with the wind blowing in his face.

"I thought you said you were going to let me go," said J-Ice as he looked at the ground six stories below.

"I am. I just never said where I was going to let you go. Have a safe trip, nigga. Tell the devil I said what's up."

Darrell put his suit coat back on and walked away. His men pushed J-Ice off the ledge. He screamed like a little girl and flailed his arms in the air. Everything slowed down for a moment and he felt as though he was flying. Then the ground came rushing up to meet him. His body burst like an overripe orange when it hit the hard concrete. The L-Block Boys were no more.

25

Detective Thomas sat in Chief Kincaid's office sweating his ass off. He had been getting yelled at for the last twenty minutes and it didn't look like the chief was getting tired anytime soon. The city was in complete chaos. Known criminals were turning up dead all over the city and no arrests were being made.

"What the fuck is going on? We have thirteen unsolved murders in the last week alone. We even have fat, naked gang leaders taking swan dives off abandoned warehouses. Where are the suspects? Why haven't there been any arrests?"

Chief Kincaid's eyes were bulging out of his head and his face was bright red. Malik hoped he would just have a heart attack and die. Anything was better than being yelled at by him. Plus his breath smelled of

David Givens

onions and liverwurst.

"Well sir, no one is talking. People are scared. There isn't a lot of evidence either. These guys know what they are doing."

"I don't want to hear that shit. Who gives a fuck if people are scared? If they opened their mouths and talked then they wouldn't have to be scared anymore. You are just pissing around chasing your own tail when you need to be out there solving something. The mayor is on my ass right now and if he is on my ass then I'm damn sure going to be on yours. Now get the fuck out of my sight and do your goddamn job!"

"Fucking asshole," Malik mumbled as he rose to his feet and turned to leave.

"What was that?"

"Nothing sir, just was thinking out loud about possible suspects."

"Just get your ass out in the streets and make something happen."

Detective Thomas slammed the chief's door and walked back to his desk. He was tired of being yelled at like he was a child. The GMC was destroying the other crews in the city and he didn't have a shred of evidence to prove it. The chief wouldn't give the approval for surveillance on Darrell Jenkins or Terry Law without really strong evidence. So now the he was forced to wait around and see if they slipped up.

There had been no more calls from the anonymous caller, but he was sure there would be more. He just wished that they would hurry up already. There would have to be a break in the case soon or he would be looking for another job. Time was not on his side.

* * * *

Across town Keke sat in her living room watching Judge Hatchett on her television. She was also on the phone talking to one of her many girlfriends while painting her toenails at the same time. Darrell Jr. was outside on the sidewalk riding his Big Wheel. Keke had her window open with the blinds pulled up so she could keep an eye on him.

She wasn't really looking at him since her television was in the other direction. In fact, she let him play alone in the front yard by himself all the time. People in the neighborhood knew he was the Sandman's son so she wasn't concerned about anyone doing something to him. Besides, it wasn't like she really cared anyway.

To her he was just a means to stay close to Darrell. As long as she had his son, he would have to give her money and associate with her. Every chance she got, she took advantage of the situation. She knew if she could get him alone she could put the pussy on him. If she put it on him enough he would come to his senses

David Givens

and realize that she was the woman he was supposed to be with.

She was the one that was with him when he was dead broke. He couldn't blame her for fucking Big Rome on the low. She just needed more financial freedom than he could give her at the time. It was just business. Now that he had the funds to secure the type of lifestyle she wanted she was determined to get back into his good graces.

A couple months ago she had put her plan into motion. She would always make sure to wear something sexy when Darrell came over. Sometimes she would call him with bogus emergencies just so he would come over. Once she got him alone, it was on and popping. He just couldn't resist her head game. She knew she was getting close to breaking him down when the unthinkable happened.

That Sherrice bitch showed up out of the blue and ruined everything. She stole Keke's dream in the blink of an eye. To make matters worse, she whipped her ass on top of it. Darrell wouldn't even come in the house anymore. His lawyer even sent over papers about taking full custody. He was done with her and she knew it.

It was okay though. She wasn't going to let her son go without a fight. That extra grand a month came in handy. Besides, she was getting the last laugh on

David Givens

Darrell anyway. She had been fucking his boy Terry for a little over a year. It had started out as a drunken one night stand and blossomed into something else.

If she couldn't have her number one option then she would have to go with number two. There was no need for her to suffer if Darrell didn't want her. She needed a sponsor to keep her laced up and ahead of the other broke hoodrats out there. Terry was just the man to do it.

She liked the danger that surrounded Terry. Darrell was dangerous in his own way, but Terry was cocky with it. He just didn't give a fuck. Plus, he loved tossing around money like it was nothing. That was the type of man she needed in her life. She was going to have to lock him down. The look on Darrell's face would be priceless when she started showing up places with his boy.

Darrell Jr. sat on his Big Wheel slapping at the annoying flies circling his head and being bored. He didn't have many friends to play with since his mother was known to all the children on the block as the mean lady. She was always yelling about something and acting crazy. He sometimes thought she was an alien. That would explain why she barely talked to him and sucked sugar up her nose. Only an alien would do something like that.

David Givens

His eyes lit up when he saw the ice cream truck coming around the corner. The smile on his face disappeared quickly when he realized he wouldn't be getting any ice cream. He knew his mother wouldn't give him any money if he asked. She never bought him any treats. He shoved his hand in his pocket and pouted.

His hand brushed up against a crinkled piece of paper in his pocket. He pulled it out and realized it was a one dollar bill. It must have been from the last time he was at his Dad's house. Lucky his mother wasn't too keen on doing the laundry on time. He knew he could get some ice cream now.

He looked back at the house to see if his mother was watching. Of course she was too busy talking on the phone and looking at the television to notice him as usual. He knew he wasn't supposed to cross the street, but he really wanted some ice cream. The truck was almost past his house, too. Without a second thought, he pedaled down the driveway and out into the street.

Keke was engrossed in the television show she was watching. Some fat bitch was on the show telling the Judge that she was 100 percent sure some funny looking nigga was her babydaddy. The man was saying the baby didn't look like him so he wasn't claiming it. When the judge read the results of the DNA test and said the baby wasn't his, the man damn near started

David Givens

break dancing.

"I don't know why that nigga celebrating. Nobody want a baby with his ugly ass. That bitch should be slapped for fucking with him in the first place. Unless he got big bank there ain't no reason to let him hit any skins," said Keke to her friend on the other end of the phone. "These bitches will fuck anything nowadays. If it ain't about the cheddar I can do better."

Suddenly, the sound of screeching tires could be heard over the television. It was followed by a noise that sounded a lot like a soccer ball after David Beckham kicked it really hard. That's when the screams started. Keke turned around, annoyed that her show was being interrupted by some drama happening out on her street.

"Darrell, get your ass in here!" Keke shouted. When he didn't answer, she hung up the cordless on her friend and walked toward the door. She was going to beat his little ass if he wasn't in the yard.

The scene that unfolded in front of her when she walked outside took her breath away. Darrell Jr. lay out in the street covered in blood. His Big Wheel was crushed underneath the tires of a pickup truck ten feet away. People had begun to gather around and point. Some skinny-ass white woman in a plaid dress was screaming hysterically while her husband held her.

David Givens

Soon Keke's own screams were joining hers.

* * * *

Darrell was across town in his master bedroom getting his freak on when his house phone rang. Sherrice was riding him like he was the last man on Earth, so he wasn't trying to answer shit. It was taking all of his will power not to cum too soon. The way she was putting it on him made it a hard task.

The phone stopped ringing then it started up again. Darrell reached for the cordless phone that was somewhere buried in the covers. Sherrice shot him a dirty look as he located it and picked it up. Keke's cell phone number showed up on the caller ID. Sherrice grabbed the phone out of his hand, looked at the number, and tossed the phone to the other side of the room. She was not about to have a great session of afternoon sex ruined by his ghetto-ass babymomma.

Sherrice bent down and bit Darrell's nipple hard. He responded by thrusting his dick further up into her. She let out a gasp as it felt like he was hitting one of her kidneys. His long stroke was definitely the death stroke. She could feel her orgasm building steam. Just as she was about to explode, Darrell's cell phone started blowing up on the stand next to the bed.

"Don't you answer that shit, nigga," Sherrice said through clenched teeth.

David Givens

"Let me just see who it is." Darrell grabbed his phone and saw Keke's cell phone number again. "It must be an emergency cause she knows not to blow my phones up like this. Let me get this."

"It better be an emergency or you about to have one up in here," she said as she tightened her pussy muscles around Darrell's dick.

Darrell had to fight back a moan as he hit the answer button on his cell. After a few seconds of listening, his whole demeanor changed. Sherrice could feel his dick going soft inside her. His eyes filled with an emotion she had never saw before. Panic was written all over his face.

"I'll be there right away." Darrell slid from under Sherrice so quick she almost fell off the bed and onto the floor.

"What's going on, baby?" Sherrice asked as she watched him racing around the room throwing his clothes back on.

"Darrell Jr. was hit by a car. I'm going to meet his mother at the emergency room."

"Oh shit, I'm coming with you."

"Then hurry up and get dressed. I'm trying to be out the door like yesterday."

Sherrice jumped up and ran to the closet. She grabbed a black tank top and a pair of blue jeans.

David Givens

Darrell raced past her with his shirt on backwards still buttoning up his pants. By the time she put on some sandals and sprayed on some perfume to cover up the smell of sex, Darrell already had the Benz backed out of the garage. She hopped in the passenger seat and they sped off toward the hospital praying that his son was okay.

26

Darrell turned into the Covenant Medical Center emergency room parking lot doing about eighty. He barely avoided hitting the building as he slammed on the brakes, stopping within inches of the automated doors. Sherrice was by his side as he ran into the emergency room looking for Keke. They found her sitting off in the corner by herself crying with a box of tissues.

"What the hell happened?" Darrell's voice was full of emotion.

To Sherrice's dismay, Keke jumped up and ran into Darrell's arms. She began to tell him a sad story about a reckless driver hitting their son while she tried to cross the street to get some ice cream with him. The whole time she cried and buried her face in Darrell's chest wetting up his shirt. He absentmindedly stroked

David Givens

her hair while he consoled her.

Sherrice tried not to be furious, but the whole scene was a bit much. Plus, Keke's story had so many holes in it that it was ridiculous. She swore the bitch winked at her over Darrell's shoulder. Sherrice was about to break up the touching family moment when they were interrupted by an older white lady wearing a gray pantsuit.

"Hello, I'm looking for a Miss Kendra Alexander."

Keke took her face from Darrell's chest and stared hard at the woman. "That's me, what can I do for you?"

"My name is Mrs. Young. I work for the Department of Human Services. I'm here to talk to you about your son."

"What do you need to talk to me about my son for?" Keke put a lot of attitude in her voice and rolled her eyes at the woman.

Sherrice thought it was amazing how the tears magically disappeared from Keke's eyes. Darrell screwed up his face and looked from Keke to the lady and back again. He took a step back and waited for what was coming next. Somehow he knew he wasn't going to like it.

"Well Miss Alexander, we have been getting a lot of reports lately about you leaving your son unattended in your front yard. I was on my way to your house to meet with you when I came upon the accident. It's very unfor-

David Givens

tunate that your son was hit by a car, but what I find more disturbing is that I stood outside with your neighbors for a couple of minutes before you even came out of your house to see what was wrong."

"You must be mistaken, bitch. I never leave my son unattended. I was in the window watching him and I called out to him to stop him from going in the street, but it was too late. The only reason it took me so long to get outside was that I was in such a rush to get to him that I fell and hurt my ankle." Keke started limping on the ankle that she had just walked perfectly on two seconds ago.

"You just told me you were outside with him crossing the street when some crazy driver came out of nowhere," Darrell said, folding his arms across his chest.

Keke was caught in a lie and she knew it. *Why didn't the little brat just stay in the yard?* Now there was some old bitch all in her mix and her babydaddy was probably about to wild out. Lucky for her, the doctor showed up so she didn't have to answer any questions right away.

"I'm looking for the parents of Darrell Jenkins Junior?" asked the young Indian doctor. His hairless face made him look too young to be practicing medicine.

"I'm his father," stated Darrell.

David Givens

"I'm Dr. Guswami. Your son has sustained massive head trauma. We got the bleeding to stop and the swelling to go down somewhat. It will take some time before we know if he has suffered any brain damage. He also has a punctured lung and a broken arm. His vital signs are strong at the moment, but he has lost a lot of blood. Unfortunately, we are short on his blood type. I need someone to donate some blood so we can keep him stabilized."

Darrell and Keke followed the doctor back into the OR. Mrs. Young informed Keke she would be waiting for her when she came back. Sherrice was left standing by Mrs. Young trying to process all the information that had just passed back and forth in front of her.

The doctor led Darrell and Keke into two separate rooms. Some nurses came in later and drew blood from both of them. They were informed that the samples would be tested right away to determine which one of them matched their son's blood type. The nurses said they should have the results in about fifteen minutes. Both parents went back out into the waiting room to wait.

Darrell was pissed at Keke, but he knew now wasn't the time to get at her. He was more concerned with his son's well being. There would be plenty of time to yell at her later. If his son was brain damaged then yelling wasn't all that he would do.

When Keke came into the waiting area, Mrs. Young escorted her over to a couch on the other side of the waiting room to talk to her in private. Sherrice noticed that their conversation didn't appear to be going too well judging by the look on Keke's face. She was all frowned up and gesturing wildly with her hands. The older social worker just kept on talking to her in hushed tones like she was used to ghetto-ass parents snapping on her all the time.

Darrell sat down next to Sherrice and put his head in his hands. He felt angry and powerless all at the same time. Sherrice rubbed his back and did her best to comfort him. She didn't have any experience in this type of situation so she didn't know what to say.

Darrell couldn't take it anymore and went up the front desk. "Excuse me, but would it be okay if I just looked in on my son for a moment?"

The woman at the front desk took down his name then she got on the phone. She held a short conversation with someone on the other end then hung up. Since his son was stabilized at the moment Darrell could go and visit with him for a few minutes. She told him what room to go to.

Darrell grabbed Sherrice's hand and took her down the hallway with him. They came to the third room on

David Givens

the right and entered. Darrell Jr. lay in the hospital bed looking like a science experiment gone wrong. He had tubes going in and out of his body as well as a cast on his arm. Various machines were hooked up to him monitoring his vital signs. His skin looked almost like plastic. Darrell almost broke down seeing his little man like that.

He vowed in his head that he would do everything in his power to get full custody. From today's events it didn't look like he would have to work too hard. He bent over and kissed his son on the forehead. Sherrice was moved by the gesture and had to blink back tears.

They walked back out into the waiting area to see Keke shedding more tears. These ones looked more like tears of anger than hurt. Her anger was aimed toward Mrs. Young. The two stood toe-to-toe.

"You can't take my son from me, bitch. You motherfuckers always be harassing black folks. Why don't you go after the guy that was driving the truck?" Keke was all up in the social worker's face.

"We can and we will take your son, Miss Alexander. It's obvious to me that you neglect your son on a daily basis. I'll recommend to the judge tomorrow morning that your son be released to us pending an investigation of the allegations against you. For your sake, I would get a good lawyer. You may face criminal charges of neglect or child endangerment." Miss Young didn't seem to be fazed by or scared of Keke's antics one bit.

"You can place him in my custody," Darrell spoke up.

"Well if you come down to the courthouse tomorrow at eight when I make my recommendation you can state your claim, Mr. Jenkins. You seem like a nice man. I don't see why the judge wouldn't place him with you during the interim."

"I'll be there with my lawyer."

"Hell naw, this shit can't be happening. I was set up." Keke was highly upset. No one knew she was really mad about the money.

While all the commotion was going on, a nurse appeared. She had a very serious look on her face. Everyone stopped what they were doing and looked at her when she cleared her throat. Sherrice rolled her eyes.

"There seems to be a situation of a sensitive nature. The doctor requests to see you, Mr. Jenkins."

Darrell and Sherrice followed the nurse to a small office located next to the vending machines. Dr. Guswami sat behind a desk suddenly looking very old. He had the nurse close the door so they could have some privacy. It took him a moment to finally speak.

"I have something that may be very painful that I have to share with you, Mr. Jenkins. Do you wish me to

David Givens

tell you in front of your girlfriend?"

"Go ahead, I share everything with her."

"We got the results back from testing Miss Alexander's blood and your blood. Your son's blood type is O positive. Miss Alexander's blood type is B positive while yours is AB negative. So we still need a donor."

"Why wouldn't my blood be a match for my son?"

"I'm sorry to inform you, but Darrell Junior is not your biological son."

Sherrice was stunned and sat with her mouth hanging open. Darrell sat there staring at the doctor for a moment. His breathing started to get heavier. The look in his eyes made the doctor jump back in his chair. Sherrice reached for Darrell's hand, but he snatched it away. In a flash, he burst out the door and was going down the hallway.

Keke was sitting on the couch still reeling over the fact that she might have to go to jail for someone else hitting her child with a truck. She looked up and saw Darrell coming toward her with Sherrice running behind him. The look on his face was straight murderous.

Darrell was full of rage and could barely contain it. He walked over to the couch and in one swift motion he gave Keke a backhand so hard her head almost flew off

David Givens

then he wrapped his huge hands around her neck and lifted her clean off the couch. People panicked and ran for cover. Sherrice was next to him telling him to stop, but her voice sounded so far away. All he could think about was the fact that he had been bonding with another nigga's son for the last three years. The bitch had played him before and now it was happening all over again.

"Who is Darrell Junior's fucking dad, bitch? Did you think you could get away with playing me for a fool?"

Keke wasn't able to answer him. His hands had cut off all oxygen to her lungs. Her eyes bulged out of her head while her feet kicked in the air almost a full foot off the ground. She tried to beat on his arms, but it was no use. They were hard as steel.

"Darrell let her go, now! She is not worth it, baby. I know you're hurt, but don't ruin your life over it." Sherrice tried to reason with him.

Darrell snapped out of his trance and dropped Keke to the floor. She lay on the carpet coughing and trying to take in as much air as she could. Her vision was blurry and her ass hurt from where she hit the floor. She couldn't believe he had almost choked the living shit out of her.

"Tell me who Darrell Junior's father is or I'll kill your ass right here!"

David Givens

"It can only be one other person. I was only with you and Big Rome during the time I got pregnant," said Keke in between coughs.

"I thought you started fucking him later?"

"I lied. I just always assumed Darrell Junior was yours because I was with you more."

Darrell looked at her as if he was truly seeing the real her for the first time. His whole relationship with her had been a lie. The bitch had played him from the start. He wished he would have listened to his friends that warned him about her a long time ago. If there weren't so many witnesses around he would be tempted to get his gun out of the car and empty a few clips into her trifling ass.

"Bitch, I'm going to tell you this one time so you better listen real good. Don't you ever in your life talk to me again. Don't look in my direction when you see me or even fix your mouth to say my name. You are dead to me." Darrell's voice had so much venom in it that Keke actually jumped back as if the words had physically slapped her.

Sherrice could feel Darrell's pain. She had never liked Keke before, but she damn sure hated the bitch now. As much as she would have liked to see him kick her ass up and down the hospital it wouldn't change a thing. The best thing to do would be to never talk to her

David Givens

again. She didn't have a reason to be in Darrell's life anymore.

"Baby, why don't you go home and lie down. I'll be home shortly," said Sherrice.

"What are you going to stick around for?"

"Well there is still a young boy in there who needs blood and it just so happens that I'm his blood type."

"You would do that even though he is not my son?"

"How could you say such a thing? He is still a human being. I'm not that bogus."

"I'm sorry, that's just my anger talking. You go ahead and do that. I'll leave the car here with you and walk home."

"Are you sure?"

"Yeah, I need to clear my head."

When Darrell left the hospital security guards finally showed up like they really would have done something. Sherrice laughed at the nerdy flashlight cops. They would have needed more than pepper spray to handle Darrell. Sherrice took one last look down at Keke, who was being helped up off the floor by one of the security guards. She pitied her more than anything else. Without so much as a second glance she went off to find the nurse so she could give blood and save a life.

David Givens

27

Darrell was distant for the next few days. He stayed out a lot and came in drunk at times. Sherrice gave him his space. She knew he had to work through whatever he was going through. When the time was right he would come to her.

On the fourth day, Sherrice came down to the kitchen to find him sitting at the table drinking coffee and reading the newspaper. He was sober and the stubble that had grown on his face was trimmed back into a nice looking goatee. The lost look he had in his eyes was gone. The Sandman was back.

"I'm not going to see him again," he said without looking up.

"Not going to see who?" Sherrice knew what he was going to say, but she hoped he would reconsider.

"The boy who I thought was my son. I know it may seem harsh, but I would never be able to raise him knowing who his father was. It would make me treat him differently. He is better off with a good family."

"But..."

"That's my decision. I'll talk about the subject no more."

And like that the subject was done. Darrell went back to his paper and Sherrice went out to shop. She didn't agree with him, but it wasn't her decision to make. It was just good to have him back to normal again.

* * * *

Keke, on the other hand, was anything but normal. She sat alone in her dark living room with barely any clothing on listening to Anthony Hamilton on her sound system. Her hair was straight up raggedy and she hadn't washed her ass in days. She was coked up so high she didn't even know she if she was coming or going.

Her life was in shambles. The court had taken away her son and charged her with criminal neglect. Her public defender informed her that her best option would be to cop a plea and do a few days in jail followed by two to three years of probation. She couldn't even go outside without her neighbors staring at her and shaking their heads. All them judgmental mother-fuckers could go to hell for all she cared.

She couldn't talk to Darrell anymore and Terry wasn't answering his phone all of a sudden. The nerve of that motherfucker. It wasn't supposed to end up like this. Now she was truly all alone.

She reached for a glass on her coffee table and drank its contents in one big gulp. The gin mixed with cranberry juice hit her just right. She knew she was fucking up, but she didn't care. Her rent was paid up for another month and she had a little money left in the bank. Maybe it was time for her to actually go out and get a job. She wasn't trying to face that reality just yet. For now she would let Anthony's gruff, soulful voice take her to another place.

Suddenly, she noticed for the first time that her sound system was off. *Did I remember pay the electricity bill this month?* Then one of the shadows moved. She jumped a little, but then she calmed down. The coke must have had her hallucinating. It was some good shit.

Then the shadow moved again and she knew someone was in the room with her. She jumped up terrified, but the shadowy figure gave her a backhand that knocked her back down onto the couch. The blow sobered her up a little bit. She was about to start yelling

David Givens

until she saw the gun pointed in her direction. It had a silencer on the end, so she knew whoever it was meant business.

"What do you want?" she asked in a timid voice.

The mystery person didn't answer her question. Instead the person stepped forward into the little light that was coming into the room. Keke could see that the person was wearing a mask with a smiley face on it. The mask made her tremble even more.

"Did Darrell send you? Tell him I'm sorry," Keke pleaded. "I never meant to hurt him. You got to believe me."

Her begging got her another backhand across the face. This time with the butt end of the gun. She saw stars in her eyes as she reeled from the blow. A small trickle of blood ran down her face. Then she heard a voice that sounded cold as ice.

"You fucked up, bitch. People like you make me sick. You couldn't even be a halfway decent mother to your son."

"Fuck you! How dare you judge me. You don't know me." Keke was crying now.

"Oh I know you. Little whores like you come a dime a dozen. You don't care who you hurt. It's all about your selfish needs. You're pathetic."

"Who the hell are you?"

David Givens

The mysterious figure took the mask off and looked Keke square in the face. She fell off the couch and started laughing hysterically. This had to be some sick type of joke. Her laughter died in her throat as the gun rose in her direction once again. Two shots and her world went black.

The stranger put away the gun and looked down at Keke's lifeless body. She had been an unexpected hitch in the plan. However, her death would prove to be very useful in the overall scheme of things. The stranger stepped over her body and turned the sound system back on. Anthony Hamilton's melodic voice filled the silent room once again.

28

Darrell was waiting inside the car wash he owned while his employees detailed his Lexus truck. Besides the fact that he found out his son wasn't his, he was having a good week. The GMC had successfully taken over all the neighborhoods around the Logan Avenue area that the L-Block Boys once controlled. The other crews had taken notice and new people were joining the team day and night. The money was flowing like Patrón in a rap video.

Lo-Key was making a little noise out in the City View area, but it was nothing. His boys had done a few erratic drive-bys that only resulted in a little property damage. Darrell was kind of surprised by Lo-Key's attempted hardcore response. Everyone knew he was an imaginary gangsta. Too much BET and not enough common sense. He would be dealt with soon enough.

The only other problem was the Crazy White Boys. They continued to come into the community and sell Meth like nothing was wrong. Darrell took it as a sign of disrespect. Their leader had even put the word out that he wasn't going anywhere. In so many words he had told Darrell to go fuck himself. That alone earned him a special spot in Darrell's heart. A spot reserved for a soon-to-be dead man.

Darrell glanced up just in time to see Detective Thomas enter his place of business. He really wasn't in the mood for his bullshit. The two cops that came in behind him didn't go unnoticed though. Whatever he was there about it probably wasn't good news.

"Hey, Darrell, I have a few questions for you. Do you mind if we go into the back office?"

Darrell ushered him into the tiny back office that was normally used by the manager. He had a funny feeling that he was not going to like what came out of the detective's mouth next.

"So Darrell, where were you yesterday morning?"

"What the fuck does that have to do with anything?"

"A murder investigation. Now where were you yesterday morning?"

"After breakfast I went down to the recording studio to work with some new talent. I didn't get done down there until around noon."

"Can anyone vouch for you on that?"

"Around ten people were in the studio. I can give you their names and numbers if you like. I can even get you the surveillance tapes from the security cameras. Now what the hell is this about a murder?"

"I'll need all that information from you before the day is over. By the way, Kendra Alexander was found murdered. She had been dead since yesterday morning."

"What!" Darrell stood up from his seat and stared at the detective in disbelief. There had to be some mistake. "You are bullshitting me, right?"

"I'm afraid not. You're also the number one suspect. I heard about the little altercation you had with her at the hospital after you found out your son really wasn't your son. I'm betting that really burned you up inside."

"Fuck you. I didn't kill her. I'll have my lawyer get you all the information you need about my whereabouts yesterday. This conversation is over. Get the fuck out of here."

"No need to get all emotional. I'm just doing my job." Detective Thomas smirked as he got to his feet. "If any of your information doesn't check out I'll be back for your black ass. Have a good day."

Darrell watched the detective leave. This shit could-

David Givens

n't possibly be happening now. Besides him, who would want to see Keke dead? It didn't make any sense. Someone was setting him up. The uneasy feeling he had a few weeks ago was creeping back up on him.

He left the car wash before his truck was fully done and went back to the house. Sherrice was at work, so he would have the house to himself. When he got inside, he checked his mail which the maid stacked neatly everyday on the kitchen counter. He noticed a large manila envelope with no return address at the bottom of the pile.

His hands shook as he opened the envelope. It contained a set of back and white 8x10 photos. The images on them made him stagger back against the sink. What the fuck was going on? Anger and confusion washed over him in waves.

He grabbed his keys and rushed out the door. In a second he was back out on the street pushing his Lexus to the limit. He ran stop signs and red lights on the way to his destination. His chrome Desert Eagle lay on the seat next to him ready for action. Finally, he stopped in front of a huge house on the upper east side.

The gun gleamed in the sunlight as he hopped out his truck and left it running. He tucked the gun in his pants as he reared back and kicked the front door. It

David Givens

took him three kicks before the deadbolt gave way. The music was so loud in the house that no one heard him enter. He raced through the living room and bounded down the stairs headed for the basement. The manila envelope was tucked tightly under his arm.

He entered the fully furnished basement and looked around. Marijuana smoke clouded the air while Young Jeezy's voice boomed through subwoofers as big as refrigerators. He walked through the haze and past countless arcade games. In the next room he found who he was looking for.

Terry was buck naked lying on a pool table with three fine-ass project bitches servicing him. They were also naked and snorting coke off of various parts of his body. The man was truly a freak and a half. Darrell pulled out his gun and shot the stereo. This little party was about to officially get shut the fuck down.

The bitches started screaming until Darrell told them to shut the fuck up. The huge gun and his deep voice were more than enough to make them chill out real quick. Terry sat up and had the nerve to smile at him like this was an everyday occurrence. Either he was really high or just plain crazy like everyone said.

"You hoes need to bounce. I have some business to discuss with my guy here." Darrell waved toward the door with his gun. The girls grabbed their stuff and ran

David Givens

out the basement like it was on fire.

"So what happened to knocking on the door like a normal brother?" Terry put his pants on and looked at Darrell like he was funny. The man was high as a kite.

Darrell tucked his gun away and walked up on his friend as if he didn't know him. He wasn't in the mood to be funny. His first punch lifted Terry up into the air. His next one drove him back down into the floor. He gave him a few open hand slaps to loosen him up. Then he slung him over into a chair in the corner and pulled his gun out again.

"What that hell is wrong with you, nigga?" Terry spit out blood and wiped his mouth with the back of his hand.

"You know Keke was found murdered this morning?"

"Naw, but what the hell that got to do with me?"

"This, motherfucker," Darrell said as he threw the manila envelope at Terry. One end was open so the photos flew out and landed everywhere. Images of Terry fucking Keke in various positions littered the floor.

"How the fuck did you get those?" asked Terry as his eyes grew larger than they already were.

"Maybe I should be asking you that question. Of all people, why would you fuck with her? You knew she was supposed to be my babymomma."

"One thing just led to another. You know how it is. I wanted to tell you, but I knew you would trip. At least she turned out not to be your babymomma."

"You don't get it do you, motherfucker?"

"Get what? She was a lying-ass bitch that played everyone and gave good head. She's gone now so why you tripping?"

Darrell came closer with his gun aimed at Terry's balls. "You know I'm the number one suspect because of that shit that went down at the hospital the other day? First this bitch ends up dead and then someone sends me photos of you screwing her. What the fuck is going on?"

"I don't know, man. That shit sounds crazy to me too."

"I just got one question for you. Did you kill her?"

"Fuck no, nigga. What the hell would I gain out of killing her? That bitch gave me some of the best head I ever had."

Darrell searched Terry's eyes for the truth. He knew in his heart that his boy was being honest. It still didn't change the fact that he had been hitting Keke off on the low. He didn't know if he could look at him the same anymore. If Terry kept that from him, there's no telling what else he was hiding.

David Givens

"This is all some crazy shit. Someone is playing games with me. I don't like games." Darrell lowered his gun and rubbed his temple with his free hand.

"I don't like games that involve me either. Someone took those pictures cause I sure in the hell didn't. It's got to be someone close to us. I'm a check some niggas out."

"I guess we just have to watch each other's backs from now on. Sorry about your stereo. I'll get a new one sent over."

"That's cool, nigga. Just don't ever put your hands on me or point a gun at me again. I just might forget we friends."

"That's fair enough."

Both men stared each other down for a moment. They both knew in the back of their minds that their friendship would never be the same. Darrell backed out of the room never taking his eyes off Terry. When he was gone Terry got up and kicked his pool table until his leg was sore. He wasn't really all that mad about getting his ass kicked. He was just pissed that he had wasted all that top quality cocaine on those hoes and didn't get to finish his private party.

An hour later, Terry was still in his basement cleaning up. He turned around quickly when he felt a presence. A lone figure stepped out the shadows wearing a

David Givens

smiley face mask. Terry stuck up his finger and kept sweeping with his broom.

"You sent him those fucking pictures, didn't you?"

"They serve a purpose in my master plan," said the stranger.

"Don't you think you could have warned me first? Look at my fucking lip. That mother fucker could have killed me."

"I knew he wouldn't. Just trust me. Before long you will be the leader of the GMC and control the whole city. Isn't that what you deserve?"

"You damn right. I've been putting in work for a long time. My name is ringing in the streets more than the Sandman's. Niggas fear me. I just want what's due to me. Why can't I just smoke that nigga? It would be a lot easier."

"Cause I'm not through with him yet. There would be no satisfaction in just killing him now. We have to wait until the GMC is in a position to take over first."

"What the hell are you getting out of this?"

"That's my business. You just stick to the plan."

"Alright, by the way, what's up with the whole wearing a mask and using a device to change your voice thing? You the Phantom of the Opera or something?"

"Don't ask questions you really don't want to know the answers to. Just do your job and you'll be reward-

David Givens

ed. I'll keep in touch."

Terry shrugged his shoulders and kept sweeping. The stranger was starting to get on his nerves with all that secret identity bullshit. Real niggas did things out in the open. However, if the plan panned out the way it was supposed to then he would be running things. He was tired of living in the Sandman's shadow. It was time for Terry Law to shine for once.

29

Darrell needed some time away after his lawyer got the cops to back up off him about the Keke murder case. His alibi checked out, so Detective Thomas had to leave him alone. Sherrice didn't like the nappy-headed detective at all. He kept staring at her strangely and asking her if he had met her before. In that nigga's dreams.

Sherrice came into the bedroom and kicked off her black Giuseppe shoes, and lay down on her bed for the first time in two weeks. Darrell had taken her on a trip to New York and they had just gotten back. It had been one of the best experiences in her life, but she was dog tired now.

The trip had been just what they needed. Darrell had spoiled Sherrice and treated her like a queen the

David Givens

whole time. He let her go buck wild and spend up money in all the stores she had read and heard about on television—Barneys, Saks, Neiman Marcus and a slew of others. His friend Carlos had let them use his private jet so she could get all the stuff she bought back in one trip.

They also did some sightseeing while they were in town. They hit up the Empire State Building as well as the Statue of Liberty. Sherrice's favorite was when they got to visit the set of "*106 & Park*." The Young Riders were there giving their first performance since they were signed to Kanye West's label. It was great to go backstage and meet everyone.

Diddy just happened to be there promoting one of his new artists. He hit it off with Darrell and invited him and Sherrice out to dinner later that night. When they got to Justin's it was filled with celebrities and sports stars. Lil' Kim was even having a birthday bash in the back.

Later on in the evening, they partied into the wee hours at 40/40 Club. Jay-Z and Fabolous were in attendance as well as Kimora Lee Simmons and her new man. Sherrice had to admit she was star struck like a motherfucker. Darrell seemed right at home mingling with the stars, but it would take her some getting used to. She almost died laughing when Darrell had to check

David Givens

Shemar Moore for hitting on her. The brother almost pissed himself when Darrell stepped to him.

They made passionate love every night and sometimes early in the morning in the huge suite Darrell rented for the two weeks inside Trump Plaza. Once again, Darrell's friend Carlos had hooked them up. The suite was so plush and big Sherrice had to keep reminding herself that it wasn't a house. She sometimes expected to see a lawn outside instead of a hallway when she opened the door.

The crowning part of the trip was when Darrell proposed to her. Earlier in the day they had gone to Madison Square Garden to watch the Miami Heat beat up on the New York Knicks. Darrell had somehow got them past security and down by the locker room to chat with Shaq and Dwayne Wade when they came out to get on the bus. Sherrice took a picture with them so she could laugh about how much taller they were than her.

Then they had gone back to Justin's where Diddy cleared out a room in the back for them. There was a huge feast laid out on the table. Sherrice knew something was up when Brian McKnight came out the kitchen and serenaded them. His voice was so beautiful. When she turned around Darrell was down on his knee with a jewelry box in his hand. She said yes

David Givens

almost before he could finish asking her to marry him. The huge, pink, 12-carat diamond ring took her breath away.

It was the same ring she was staring at now in the comfort of her own bedroom. Tears formed in her eyes as she thought about her life. She came a long way in the last three months—from a lost little orphan to living in a big house on the hill. Rescued from the disgrace of stripping, she was running the flyest soul food restaurant in town. Life had a funny way of changing in the blink of an eye.

Darrell came up behind her and wrapped his arms around her. They lay together silently, listening to each other's heartbeats. Darrell waited until Sherrice was asleep before he got up. Like always, his mind was in overdrive thinking about the various plans he had in motion. He crept down to his study and closed the door. A few seconds later he was leaned back in his chair puffing on Cush while knocking back shots of Grey Goose.

He thought about his lovely queen sleeping down the hallway and smiled. She had his heart wrapped around her finger. He wasn't ashamed to admit that. There was something about her that made him just plain old Darrell Jenkins. She loved him and not his image or what he had, which made him want to trick

David Givens

off on her more than ever.

He had been so nervous when he proposed to her. His heart was beating so fast he thought Brian McKnight could hear it over his singing. It was really a spur of the moment type of thing. He had a top notch jewelry store ship some rings over for him to view while she was in the shower one day. When he saw the pink one he just knew he had to have it. Then he and Diddy scrambled to find a way to make the moment special. Brian just happened to be touring in the city so everything came together perfectly.

The trip had also relieved a lot of stress he was experiencing. He was hurt by finding out his son wasn't his, but he didn't want to deal with it. What was crazy was the slight pang of sadness he felt for Keke. She was a scandalous bitch who had done him wrong, but she didn't deserve to die like that. He had thought about smoking her once or twice, but he never made a move to go through with it.

Now someone had punched her card and he was betting that same someone sent him those pictures of his boy and her getting it on. That was evidence that someone was out to get him or at least fuck with him. What was the reasoning behind it all? There were so many suspects that it would take him weeks to narrow it down. It would have to be put on the back burner for

David Givens

now.

There was still a city to take over. The trip had cleared his mind and now he was ready for action. Lo-Key had to go. He had given the young punk ample time to get out the game, but sometimes when you are kind, motherfuckers want to show their ass. It was all cool though. Young homie was about to find out that real life was a lot deadlier than the movies.

The same went for Dwight Jansen and his racist-ass crew. They had gotten too cocky over the years. Wealth and arrogance would do that to you. He was going to have to knock that asshole down a peg or two. The punk thought he was safe out in the country with his guns and survivalist buddies. He was going to have to show him otherwise.

30

Lo-Key was nervous as hell. Tonight was the night he was going to take out the Sandman and Terry Law. He was going to rewrite history in the hood. People were actually going to start taking him seriously after tonight. He was really going to have a rep that he could be proud of in the streets. There would be no more snickering behind his back.

Even after he built one of the largest prostitution rings in Iowa, people still doubted him. Just cause he came from suburbia and was born with a silver spoon in his mouth. It was like reverse discrimination. He couldn't be gangsta cause he never struggled?

Now these GMC cats come along and try to push him out of the limelight. It was bad enough he had to buy overpriced cocaine from them. Then all of a sudden they want to take over and run all the illegal operations in the city? Well, it wasn't going down like that.

Lo-Key had orchestrated a few drive-bys of his own. He even had a few of his boys shoot up one of the Sandman's gas stations. No one was going to bully him. As long as he stayed out of the streets and in his secure neighborhood he was fine.

He heard about what happened to J-Ice, but that clown wasn't on the same level as him. Most of his crew was gone, but he did have few loyal soldiers like Hassan left. In fact, Hassan was the one who had come to him with the information he was using tonight to get the drop on the GMC.

The Sandman and Terry Law were supposed to be meeting a supplier in an abandoned warehouse over by Gates Park at midnight. He was going to pop up with a few of his boys and give them a little surprise. They wouldn't know what hit them. Brains triumphed over brawn any day.

Lo-Key sat in the passenger seat of a black van filled with five of his most trusted men. Hassan sat beside him driving. Another van followed them filled with seven more men. It was a small force, but they were the only ones left. Besides, it didn't take that many people to throw a surprise ambush.

He checked the automatic rifle in his hand to see if

it was loaded. Hassan scored a good gun connect who had hooked them up. Lo-Key had never fired a gun before, but he was sure it couldn't be that hard. Just aim and pull the trigger.

They pulled up a couple blocks away from the warehouse. Lo-Key's stomach was doing flip flops. His dinner from earlier was threatening to come back up. He fought down his urge to vomit and exited the van. His men did the same.

They ran through a small wooded area behind the warehouse. The shadows gave them great cover. Lo-Key felt like he was in a movie going to get the bad guys. They stopped when they got to the edge of the woods. There was the slightest glimmer of a light within the darkness of the warehouse. The GMC was actually there. This was too good to be true.

The remaining City View Clique members ran toward the back of the warehouse. They found a door that was open and slipped inside. Voices could be heard coming from the deepest part of the building. They silently moved through the hallways like ninjas. Finally, they arrived at a door that was halfway open.

A soft light glowed in the room. Lo-Key hesitated and listened. He could hear the unmistakable baritone of the Sandman's voice. He peered around the corner with sweat burning his eyes. Fear gripped him, but he

David Givens

ignored it. The room was empty, but there was a trap-door that lay open in the floor. The light and voices were coming from the room below.

This would be easier than he thought. They would just have to creep up to the trapdoor and point their guns down in the hole. A few short blasts of their guns and it would be all over. It would be like shooting fish in a barrel. He didn't know why he was scared in the first place.

He signaled his men to follow him as he crept up on the trapdoor slowly. They might have a guard in place so he had to be careful. When he got to the edge he peered over, ready to take cover if a shot rang out. What he saw at the bottom of the ladder confused him at first. A walkie talkie lay on the dirt floor with a pow-erful flashlight next to it. Had the guard taken a break?

When a huge overhead light came on above them he knew it was a trap. The walkie-talkie and flashlight were decoys to lure him and his boys into the room. The door they came through slammed shut and locked. When he shielded his eyes and looked up he saw the Sandman and Terry Law looking down at him from a loft up above. They had about thirty men with them. Each was carrying an automatic assault rifle.

Lo-Key looked to his side to see if Hassan was as afraid as he was. However, Hassan was nowhere to be

David Givens

found. That bastard set him up. He wasn't going out like no punk though. He aimed his gun at the Sandman and squeezed the trigger. Too bad nothing happened. His men started to panic around him as they realized their guns were dummies, too. Hassan really got him good.

"Damn, you sure look stupid down there waving that toy gun around," said Hassan as he appeared next to Darrell.

"Hassan, you bastard! How the fuck you gone set me up? You my boy. Haven't I always treated you fair?"

"Fair ain't got shit to do with it, homie. I just chose the winning side. You should have just joined them instead of acting all tough and shit. Ain't nothing to be gained by being dead."

"My thoughts exactly," said Terry as he pointed his gun at Hassan's head.

The automatic gunfire was loud inside the abandoned warehouse. Hassan's head exploded into pieces as the bullets tore through his skull. Blood sprayed down onto Lo-Key's face. Hassan's headless body took a step then fell off the loft and landed at Lo-Key's feet. The wannabe gangsta jumped back in terror. He started mumbling and wiping at the blood with his T-shirt.

"What the fuck was that for?" asked Darrell as he picked an ear off the sleeve of his shirt.

David Givens

"I never liked that nigga. Finger waves are for bitch-es."

"You do have a point." Darrell shrugged then turned his attention back to Lo-Key who looked like he was going to shit himself. "What do you have to say for yourself?"

"Oh shit, oh shit, oh shit..." Lo-Key was clearly out of it.

"That's what I thought. You see, this is what hap-pens when you play gangsta. Terry, show these moth-erfuckers how it's really done," said Darrell as he looked Lo-Key square in the eyes.

Terry didn't need to be told twice. He took aim with his AK-47 and started mowing niggas down. The other GMC members did the same. The City View Clique nig-gas never had a chance. They were cut to pieces. *I should have been a doctor,* was Lo-Key's last thought before a hail of bullets turned him into human Swiss cheese.

31

The next morning, Dwight Jansen lay in his bed having a wet dream about Pamela Anderson. In his dream she was riding his dick while her luscious tittes bounced in his face. He sucked her nipples hard like he was nine month-old baby. She had just bent over so he could hit it from the back when a noise woke him from his sleep.

He cursed under his breath as he struggled to wipe the fog from his mind. When he recovered he realized what the noise was—it was one of the alarms he had set up around the perimeter of his property. Suddenly, another one started going off.

He rushed to his security room hoping it was just squirrels. This time of year those little bastards were always tripping his alarms. When he got to his security

David Givens

room he sat down in front of his many monitors to check out was going on. There were intruders on his property alright, and they weren't no damn squirrels.

Every monitor was filled with niggas. They all were armed and coming for him. He had to rub his eyes to make sure what he was seeing was true. Those little bastards! The Sandman had some balls to be coming on his turf.

Dwight quickly grabbed his phone and called over to the other houses to tell his men to wake up and get their gear together. From the looks of things they didn't have a lot of time. Those monkeys were going to pay for daring to set foot on his land. It looked like Armageddon was going to start early.

Darrell was outside lying down in the tall grass dressed in camouflage gear. He was using an old tractor for cover. The firefight between the GMC and CWB had been going on for five minutes already. Both sides lost a couple of good men. Mo-Mo and a few other GMC soldiers had been laid out already. Jay had a gunshot wound to the left thigh, but he was hanging in there.

Terry was hiding behind a tree to his right. The man had turned into a straight up lunatic. He was handling his Israeli assault rifle like a pro. Racist skinheads were falling like leaves under his steady hail of bullets.

David Givens

Darrell watched as his friend pulled a grenade from his backpack. *Where the fuck did he get that?*

A few minutes later an explosion rocked the ground as the grenade Terry threw blew up the front of one of the houses on the property. Charred body parts were landing everywhere. Darrell could only look on in amazement. It was like World War III was going on around him. Luckily they were so far out in the country, or else the police would have been all over them. They still would have to wrap this thing up before someone realized what was going on and called in the cavalry.

When Terry threw another grenade, Darrell used its explosion as cover. He ran for the tree line. Then he circled around toward the big red barn located in the middle of the property. He knew that's where the Meth lab was located.

When he got around to the back of the building he saw two men posted up with guns. They weren't looking in his direction. He stood up and shot them in the back quickly. Then he ducked back down in the grass and waited to see if anyone would come running. After five minutes he got up and ran toward the back of the building.

He opened his backpack and pulled out a huge block of C-4 plastic explosive. Terry wasn't the only one with surprises. Carlos had found some for him rather easily. It was good having a friend like him sometimes. Darrell learned how to use the material on the internet. He had painted it the same red as the farmhouse so it would blend in. Next, he attached a cell phone detonator to it. Then he skulked back into the grass.

Dwight just happened to be coming around the corner when he saw Darrell sneaking back into the grass. What the fuck was that nigga doing behind his barn? When he saw his two men laid out on the grass, he got pissed. That was it. That nigga and his monkeys had killed a lot of his friends already. It was time for him to return the favor. He silently dipped into the grass behind Darrell.

Darrell made it to a small wooded clearing off to side. He stood up and looked around. Just as he was about to use his walkie-talkie to see where Terry was, he heard a twig snap behind him. He turned just in time to see a fist coming for his face. He turned with the blow, but the momentum still knocked him down.

"Looks like you a dead nigga now," said Dwight as he pointed his gun at Darrell. He made Darrell toss all his guns to the side and put his hands up.

"Go ahead and shoot me you pussy. I'd whip your ass without that gun and you know it."

"What did you say to me, boy?"

"You heard me. I'd kick the shit out of you. Without

that gun you're just another scary-ass cracker."

"You fucking nigga! I don't need a gun to kill you. I'll tear you apart with my bare hands!" Dwight tossed his gun to the side and ripped off his shirt exposing his heavily muscled up torso.

He had to outweigh Darrell by at least twenty pounds. Darrell got to his feet and circled the shorter, thicker man. Dwight shot forward quickly and scooped Darrell up by the legs. He slammed him to the ground hard. Darrell rolled with the impact and tossed the crazed man off him.

They both got back to their feet. Dwight threw a haymaker that Darrell blocked. Then the Sandman did what he did best. He hit Dwight in the stomach with a few body punches that made him drop his hands. Then he came up top with a wicked uppercut that snapped his head back. Dwight staggered back, dazed.

He recovered and rushed at Darrell in a frenzy. He was going for another slam, but Darrell was ready this time. He hit Dwight in the nose with a perfectly timed knee that made his body go limp on impact. Dwight fell to the ground unconscious with a broken nose.

Darrell left him lying in the grass just like that. He could have shot him, but he wanted the racist punk to know he had been bested by a black man when he woke up. He radioed Terry and told him to retreat. Then

David Givens

he grabbed his gear and got the hell out of there.

Back on the road, Terry was pissed off. "Why did we leave? We had those skinhead motherfuckers on the ropes."

"Cause we had to get far enough away from the property so I could use this." Darrell held up a cheap-ass cell phone.

"We left so you could make a fucking phone call?"

When their caravan of cars got around ten miles away Darrell entered a number into the cell phone and pressed the send button. A second later the road shook like there was an earthquake. A few pieces of burning junk fell around their cars then everything went back to normal. Terry noticed a giant cloud of smoke in the distance disappearing in the rearview mirror.

"You are one sick motherfucker," said Terry. "My kind of guy."

Dwight woke up in the field dazed and confused. One moment he was about to kill that black son of bitch, then he was waking up with a broken nose and blood all over his face. He staggered to his feet and walked back toward his property. He didn't hear anymore gunfire so the party must have been over.

His men came up to him to see if he was okay. He brushed off their concern and told them he ran into a tree. Then he and asked them what happened. They told him the niggas just picked up and left. It sounded too odd until he remembered seeing Darrell by his farmhouse. He broke out into a run with his men following closely behind him.

When he got to the back of the farmhouse he frantically searched around. His men didn't know what he was doing so they just stared. He finally spotted what looked like a cell phone attached to the side of the barn close to the ground. Too bad it started to ring when he approached it. He felt no pain as he and all of his men were blown to atoms.

262

David Givens

32

Detective Thomas sat at his desk more pissed off than he had ever been in his entire life. After the rest of the City View Clique was found in an abandoned warehouse massacred, the FBI was called in. He was off the case and was lucky to still have a job. The chief had chewed him a new one in front of everyone. He was now on a week suspension.

He turned his computer off and headed for the door. It looked like Darrell and Terry got one over on him once again. He still couldn't help but wonder who the anonymous caller was. There was a feeling in the back of his mind that they would be calling again real soon.

Maybe he could do his own little investigation. The FBI was overrated anyway. They wouldn't find out shit just like two years ago. Yeah, his own investigation sounded nice. It was time to do some real police work.

* * * *

A few weeks passed and Darrell stood in the window looking out on his city. For the first time in months, he felt somewhat at peace. The GMC had a stranglehold on the city that it wasn't about to let go anytime soon. They now controlled all the weed, cocaine, prostitution and Meth business going on in the city. He was already thinking about getting his first private jet next year as well as buying up some prime real estate to build condos.

The Minister had met with him yesterday and gave him his blessing. They agreed to a partnership that was very lucrative for both of them. Darrell made sure the Minister got a little kickback from his illegal activities while the Minister made sure the cops didn't bother him. Everyone made money and stayed out of jail. It was a win/win situation.

Darrell's relationship with Sherrice couldn't have been better. Their wedding was scheduled to take place the following summer. They had a lavish party at his restaurant last weekend to announce their engagement. Everyone who was somebody came out to congratulate them. The Minister and the Mayor

David Givens

were in attendance. Even Kanye West and his crew showed up from the Chi. It was the social event of the summer.

There was a second private party that Darrell invited Carlos to, so he could finally meet the woman who had stolen his heart. To his surprise, Carlos and Sherrice hit it off rather nicely. Carlos took him to the side later on in the evening and told him that she was a special lady. It felt good to have his mentor tell him something he already knew.

The incident at the Dwight Jansen farm was ruled an accident. Apparently, there was a Meth lab mishap on his property that killed everyone. At least that's what the Feds speculated. There wasn't a whole lot of evidence left after the blast. The GMC couldn't be tied to anything.

The FBI also came up empty on the gang murders investigation. They were keeping the case open, but everyone knew it was futile. No one would talk and the GMC wasn't sloppy. It was the same brick wall they ran into two years ago.

The relationship between Darrell and Terry was still somewhat strained. They didn't kick it like they used to. When they got together to discuss business it was always formal. Neither man said more than he had to. They became even more distant when Terry found out Sherrice got to meet Carlos.

Keke's killer was still in the back of Darrell's mind. He still didn't have any clue who did it or what their next move would be. Everything was going so good now that he knew something bad was bound to happen.

David Givens

33

The Minister sat in his den watching a plasma screen television that took up the space of almost an entire wall. He never liked to miss his *"Law & Order."* It was his favorite show followed closely by *CSI*. He had liked to watch *"Grey's Anatomy"* at one time until they got rid of the black guy.

One bodyguard was sitting behind him in a chair by the door. The other one was out in the hallway. He looked at his watch when his show went off and signaled to the bodyguard behind him that he was tired. The man and his counterpart in the hallway followed the Minister upstairs into his bedroom. There they checked every square inch of the room before retreating back out into the hallway and leaving him alone.

He changed into his Ralph Lauren pajamas and

poured himself a drink. Then he went to his window and looked out on his sprawling estate. His land went on for acres and acres. He could see his tennis court, pool, basketball court and golf course from his window. He sucked at golf, but the course impressed some of his guests who stopped by every now and then so he kept it. The mayor and police chief were always coming over to play a round or two.

When he turned from his window he saw a person standing in the shadows of his room. It didn't surprise him. With all the sins he had secretly committed he knew someone would come for him one day. It was only a matter of time.

The Minister was a man of many appetites. He loved money, power, material things and most of all, women. There were times he would take it upon himself to sleep with many of the wives of the men in his congregation. Most of the time the men were so loyal and brainwashed by him that they would just accept it. Some were even honored.

Then there were others who didn't want to go along with the program. He paid most of them off. Some tried to blackmail him or threaten to go to the media. They would usually receive a beating at the hands of his own personal goon squad. A beating wouldn't stop a select few, so he would have to arrange for more drastic

David Givens

measures. Usually this involved a fatal accident.

"Would you like a drink?" offered the Minister as he sat down on his bed.

"That's okay. I only plan to be here for a few minutes," said the stranger.

"How have I wronged you my child?"

"This little visit really doesn't have a whole lot to do with your sins. I could care less. People deserve to get done dirty if they believe you are some kind of savior."

The stranger produced a gun with a silencer on it and pointed it at the Minister. It didn't scare him in the least. It actually wasn't the first time a gun was ever pointed at him. He just wondered how he was going to get out of this current situation.

"Then why are you here?"

"I'm just working my way down the food chain. Your death is merely part of a bigger plan."

"How much can I pay you to change your mind?"

"I don't want your money. I just want you to die."

The stranger got up and shot the Minister twice in the chest. He looked down at the large red spots spreading on his pajamas in disbelief, almost like he was surprised that he was actually dying. A crazed smile danced on his lips as he slumped backwards onto his bed. His glass tumbled to the floor where it shattered. When his bodyguards burst in they found him

David Givens

dead on his bed and the balcony doors open. The most powerful man in the city was gone.

* * * *

Darrell pulled up to his house the next afternoon and was surprised to see it was crawling with cops. He jumped out and met Sherrice at the door. She looked like a mess. Her hair was standing up on her head and her clothing was disheveled. He looked past her and saw officers tossing his expensive furniture around like it was from Costco.

"Baby, they came in about an hour ago and started tearing the place apart," Sherrice said with tears running down her face.

"I'm sure there is a good explanation for this."

Darrell wasn't worried. He never left anything incriminating in his home. There were no drugs and all the guns on the premises were registered. He didn't even keep large sums of money at the house. So what the fuck were the police doing there?

A white police officer met Darrell in his living room and showed him the search warrant. They were looking for a specific gun and some photos. It didn't make any sense to him. Then he saw Detective Malik Thomas walking toward him with a huge grin on his face. The bastard looked like a cat would just swallowed the canary.

David Givens

"Well look what I have here. This looks like a murder weapon and some hard evidence." Detective Thomas held up a 9mm with a silencer attached along with the photos of Terry and Keke together.

Earlier in the day he had received a phone call from the anonymous caller. When the voice told him that he would find the murder weapon for multiple homicides along with some photos in Darrell's basement, he almost did a back flip. It took some doing for him to get a search warrant, but he knew a crooked judge that owed him a favor. It looked like that favor just paid off.

"This is a fucking set up. That shit shouldn't be in my house." Darrell could feel the room closing in on him. Someone got him good.

"Darrell Jenkins, I'm going to have to place you under arrest for the murder of Kendra Alexander and Minister Michael Akbar," Detective Thomas sneered, slapping the cuffs on Darrell's wrist.

"I'm innocent, baby. Call my lawyer and tell him to meet me at the jail. This is all a misunderstanding," he said to Sherrice.

The police led him out of the house while Sherrice stood there shocked. She ran to the house phone and called Darrell's lawyer. Hopefully, he could get him out of this one.

David Givens

34

Darrell sat in a cold, dark jail cell wondering how he ended up in this situation. Everything was going so right and then his life flipped upside down. His trial was a mockery of justice. He had been convicted of both murders and now awaited sentencing.

He knew the deck was stacked against him when the judge ordered him held without any bond. His lawyer had argued that he didn't have a record and that he was a pillar of the community. They weren't trying to hear that shit. Someone had to pay for the death of the Minister and they had found their whipping boy.

The gun turned out to be registered to him and was covered with his fingerprints. He recognized it as the gun he used to kill Rocky and Lucky months ago. The gun was supposed to be in the landfill. He had pulled over when he was taking Sherrice to his home that night and dropped it in a random trash can behind a Family Dollar store. Someone must have followed him and took it.

That was all they needed to convict him in the Minister trial. The Keke trial was much worse. Even though his alibi checked out, they still convicted him. The gun was his and the photos proved motive. The prosecution brought in all kinds of experts who said he could have faked the surveillance tapes from his studio.

There were no plea bargains offered. It looked like Darrell was going away for the rest of his life. The pending outcome didn't bother him that much. He knew the risks when he got into the game. He just wished he knew who set him up.

The only pain he felt was for Sherrice. She had come to the trials everyday dressed to impress in support of her man. He waved and blew a kiss to her every time he entered and left the courtroom. He just wished he had more time with her. It wasn't fair.

The feeling was terrible when he heard the jury foremen reading out the guilty verdicts. All he could do was listen to Sherrice wail each time and shake his head. Where was the justice? Who did he piss off so bad that they had to do this to him?

The only good news Darrell received during his trail

David Givens

was that Detective Thomas was found dead in his home. It was ruled a suicide which baffled everyone. He had just received a recommendation from the mayor for solving the Minister case and word was that he was next in line to be chief. There was a note left in his handwriting that said he was depressed, but it all seemed fishy.

Terry ran the GMC while Darrell went through his ordeal. He reassured his friend once again that he had nothing to do with what happened. Terry visited his man in jail once a week and kept his books stacked with paper. He vowed to leave no stone unturned in his search for whoever set Darrell up.

The day before Darrell's sentencing Terry was sitting in his house behind a desk covered in a mountain of coke like the scene in *"Scarface."* He was trying to snort himself into oblivion. Guilt was eating a hole into his soul. He had helped put his boy behind bars just because he wanted to be head at the table. They had been through too much shit for him to do Darrell like that. He snorted a large mound and looked up to see the stranger in a mask standing before him.

"What the fuck do you want? You happy now?"

"Almost," said the stranger.

"What do you mean almost? What more could you possibly want?"

David Givens

The stranger sat down in a seat across from Terry and removed her mask. Terry stared at her in total disbelief. She had everyone fooled the whole time. He could only stare at her in amazement.

"Remember the night you killed Big Rome?" asked the woman sitting across from him.

"Yeah, but what the fuck does that have to do with anything?"

"He was my big brother, you piece of shit," said the woman as she quickly reached across the desk and slashed Terry's throat with the straight razor she had hidden up her sleeve.

Terry immediately grabbed at his throat and got up. Blood poured out his gaping neck wound. He tried to reach for his gun nestled in his shoulder holster, but he lacked the energy to pull it free. A crazed laugh escaped his lips before his eyes rolled back in his head and he fell across the cocaine mountain on his desk.

Darrell heard about his friend's demise the next day just before he was sentenced to life. He shed a tear for his friend and for his lost freedom. He hugged Sherrice one last time before being led away. She kissed him on the lips and told him she would always love him. He told her the same.

A few weeks later, Darrell was in the prison weight room working out after hours. Even though he was locked up, his rep and influence still allowed him certain luxuries. His lawyer was working on an appeal that had a good chance of getting him out. Apparently, the search warrant on his case was bogus. He didn't want to get his hopes up, but he was feeling good.

He also had his lawyer put most of his assets in Sherrice's name. In case he never got out he never wanted her to have to want for anything. He even told her the account numbers to some of his secret offshore accounts. She fought him every step of the way telling him he was going to get out. God, he loved that woman.

Darrell was just putting back some dumbbells when a group of five large white boys from the Aryan Brotherhood strolled in. He was really going to chew out the guards for letting them in during his paid time to have the place to himself. When he looked toward the door he realized the guards weren't there. The last guy in closed the door behind him.

"Who sent you?" asked Darrell. He knew what time it was.

"Some woman named the Queen Bee," said the one in front as he walked toward Darrell. "She's paying us top dollar to make you a memory."

The men pulled out shanks and spread out. Darrell wasn't afraid, he was just confused. Who was the

David Givens

Queen Bee? Why did she want him dead?

Darrell grabbed the closest dumbbell to him and hurled it at the nearest guy crushing him in the forehead. He fell to the ground in agony. The next guy caught one to the shoulder and dropped his shank. The other three rushed Darrell and began to stab him at will.

He refused to go down and fought back hard. One man fell to the ground with a broken collarbone. Darrell choked the life out of another one. The last one stabbed him viciously in the gut and broke the shank off in him. Darrell rewarded him by breaking his neck with the last bit of his strength.

Darrell slumped down to the floor as the life seeped out of him. It was getting hard for him to breathe. He still clung to life trying to figure out who the Queen Bee was. It didn't make any sense.

"She said to tell you this is for Big Rome," said the man on the floor with the broken collarbone.

That was the straw that broke the camel's back. Everything came together for Darrell then. He knew who had played him and why. Too bad he couldn't do a damn thing about it. His eyes closed and he fell face first onto the floor. The Sandman had gone to sleep.

David Givens

Epilogue

Sherrice lay back in the bed that she and Darrell once shared. He died over a month ago and now almost everything he owned was hers—the house, the business and the cars. Even the life insurance policy he secretly took out a couple of months ago. It was worth a cool million. She had everything except for her Prince Charming.

Then again, she never really needed one in the first place. She had been taking care of herself for years and she would continue to do so. Especially since she now ran the GMC with an iron fist. She was the Queen Bee after all.

It had all started two years ago. She was living her last year in her foster home hell when her biological brother finally caught up to her. He had been searching for her for years. Imagine her surprise when she found out her brother was the biggest baller in the city—Big Rome.

David Givens

On the night she was supposed to move in with him, he was murdered. Her spirit had almost been crushed. It wasn't fair that her brother was taken from her right after she met him. Just when she was about to enjoy the good life, it was snatched from her. She had been plotting and planning ever since to get her revenge.

It was easy to get Terry to turn on Darrell. The man was jealous of his friend, but didn't want to admit it. Killing Keke was a bonus. She was one of the main reasons her brother was dead. If she never seduced him, he would still be alive. Plus, the bitch let her nephew get hit by a truck.

Of course she had to kill Terry later since he was the one who actually killed her brother. She made Darrell suffer the most because he took her brother's spot. It wasn't enough to just kill him, he had to become him. There was no way she was going to allow that.

Killing the Minister served two purposes. It gave her a high profile murder to pin on Darrell and it also cleared the path for her to take over the city completely when he was gone. There would be no sharing of her power. She was number one.

Detective Malik Thomas had to go because he figured out who she was. He couldn't be happy with getting a couple of murder convictions. One day he called her and told her that he remembered that she was the sister

David Givens

of Big Rome. He helped Big Rome track her down. Then the little rat tried to blackmail her.

He said he could dig up some type of evidence to tie her in with the murders. That bastard must not have known who he was dealing with. Sherrice showed up at his house one day when he was getting out the shower and got the drop on him. She held his own gun up against his head while he wrote out a suicide note. He told her she wouldn't get away with it. Didn't he realize how much she had already gotten away with?

The only thing that bothered her was her feelings for Darrell. It was all supposed to be fake on her end, but a part of her really fell for him. No man had ever treated her the way that he did. She agonized over her plan many nights, but in the end blood was thicker than water. She just hoped she had done the right thing.

Sherrice got off the bed and went down the hallway to the nursery where Darrell Junior was sleeping. There was no way she was going to let her nephew grow up in a foster home like she did. Soon she would change his name to Jerome Junior. He deserved his father's name.

Since all the crazy business of revenge was finally behind her, she could concentrate on expanding the business. She wasn't content with just running Waterloo. The whole Midwest was within her sights. The Queen Bee was taking over for real.

David Givens

♛ Triple Crown Publications

Order Form
P.O. Box 247378   Columbus, OH 43224

Name	
Address	
City	
State	Zipcode

QTY	TITLES	PRICE
	A Down Chick	$15.00
	A Hood Legend	$15.00
	A Hustler's Son	$15.00
	A Hustler's Wife	$15.00
	A Project Chick	$15.00
	Always a Queen	$15.00
	Amongst Thieves	$15.00
	Baby Girl	$15.00
	Baby Girl Pt. 2	$15.00
	Betrayed	$15.00
	Black	$15.00
	Black and Ugly	$15.00
	Blinded	$15.00
	Cash Money	$15.00
	Chances	$15.00
	China Doll	$15.00

Shipping & Handling
1 - 3 Books $5.00
4 - 9 Books $9.00
$1.95 for each add'l book

Total $_____

♛ Triple Crown Publications

Order Form
P.O. Box 247378   Columbus, OH 43224

Name	
Address	
City	
State	Zipcode

QTY	TITLES	PRICE
	Chyna Black	$15.00
	Contagious	$15.00
	Crack Head	$15.00
	Crack Head II	$15.00
	Cream	$15.00
	Cut Throat	$15.00
	Dangerous	$15.00
	Dime Piece	$15.00
	Dirtier Than Ever	$20.00
	Dirty Red	$15.00
	Dirty South	$15.00
	Diva	$15.00
	Dollar Bill	$15.00
	Ecstasy	$15.00
	Flipside of the Game	$15.00
	For the Strength of You	$15.00

Shipping & Handling
1 - 3 Books $5.00
4 - 9 Books $9.00
$1.95 for each add'l book

Total $_____

Forms of accepted payment: Postage Stamps, Personal or Institutional Checks & Money Orders. All mail in orders take 5-7 business days to be delivered.

♛ Triple Crown Publications

Order Form

P.O. Box 247378   Columbus, OH 43224

Name	
Address	
City	
State	Zipcode

QTY	TITLES	PRICE
	Game Over	$15.00
	Gangsta	$15.00
	Grimey	$15.00
	Hold U Down	$15.00
	Hood Richest	$15.00
	Hoodwinked	$15.00
	How to Succeed in the Publishing Game	$15.00
	Ice	$15.00
	Imagine This	$15.00
	In Cahootz	$15.00
	Innocent	$15.00
	Karma	$15.00
	Karma II	$15.00
	Keisha	$15.00
	Larceny	$15.00
	Let That Be the Reason	$15.00

Shipping & Handling
1 - 3 Books $5.00
4 - 9 Books $9.00
$1.95 for each add'l book

Total $_____

Forms of accepted payment: Postage Stamps, Personal or Institutional Checks &
Money Orders. All mail in orders take 5-7 business days to be delivered.

♚ Triple Crown Publications

Order Form

P.O. Box 247378   Columbus, OH 43224

Name	
Address	
City	
State	Zipcode

QTY	TITLES	PRICE
	Life	$15.00
	Love & Loyalty	$15.00
	Me & My Boyfriend	$15.00
	Menage's Way	$15.00
	Mina's Joint	$15.00
	Mistress of the Game	$15.00
	Queen	$15.00
	Rage Times Fury	$15.00
	Road Dawgz	$15.00
	Sheisty	$15.00
	Stacy	$15.00
	Stained Cotton	$15.00
	Still Dirty	$20.00
	Still Sheisty	$15.00
	Street Love	$15.00
	Sunshine & Rain	$15.00

Shipping & Handling
1 - 3 Books $5.00
4 - 9 Books $9.00
$1.95 for each add'l book

Total $_____

♛ Triple Crown Publications

Order Form

P.O. Box 247378   Columbus, OH 43224

Name	
Address	
City	
State	Zipcode

QTY	TITLES	PRICE
	The Cartel's Daughter	$15.00
	The Game	$15.00
	The Hood Rats	$15.00
	The Pink Palace	$15.00
	The Reason Why	$15.00
	The Set Up	$15.00
	Torn	$15.00
	Trickery	$15.00
	Vixen Icon	$15.00
	Whore	$15.00

Shipping & Handling
1 - 3 Books $5.00
4 - 9 Books $9.00
$1.95 for each add'l book

Total $_____

Forms of accepted payment: Postage Stamps, Personal or Institutional Checks &
Money Orders. All mail in orders take 5-7 business days to be delivered.